T0370136

The Realm of Unity

V. M. ELYSE

TheRealmOfUnity.com

ISBN 979-8-35096-742-5

For Aysia
La Luz de mi Vida

Contents

Welcome to Unity 1
My New Home 9
My Story 18
Jax 26
The Three Sisters 34
Magna 37
Samita 40
Malika 45
Welcome Party 50
Maanya 54
Drake, Viola, Yeshua, and Hannah 57
Veeda 60
Education 63
The Central Hub of Elysia 71
Harmony Healing Center 76
The Radiant Domes 84
The Zephyr 94
Leadership 99
Exploring Unity 102
The Birth of Viviana 111
My Innate Gifts 116
Oriane's Revelation 121
The Newest Luminole 127
History of Unity 133
Glossary of Terms 135
Acknowledgements 137

CHAPTER ONE

Welcome to Unity

After a lifetime of chasing the slippery fish of peace, I reveled in the rainstorm of the absence of my suffering.

Standing, my feet buried in the warm sand, the salty spray clung to my skin. The cry of the seagulls, muted by the deafening roar of the waves, was like a call to come home to some unknown place. Imbued with exquisite serenity, I closed my tear-drenched eyes and raised my face to the sun. After a lifetime of chasing the slippery fish of peace while trying to navigate a sleeping world, I reveled in the rainstorm of the absence of my suffering.

The crash of the ocean faded away, replaced with an all-consuming silence. Swaying, I basked in ineffable bliss, my heart's yearning finally fulfilled. A vibration permeated my cellular structure, calling into question everything I ever thought I knew about myself. A sudden rush of vital energy raced up my spine. Every hair stood at attention. As the atoms of my form exploded, the mystery of my existence unraveled, and I dissolved into emptiness.

As my perceptions slowly reconstituted, a gentle breeze kissed my skin. The chirp of a song sparrow rang like a crystalline melody.

Filling my lungs with fresh, crisp air, the sweet fragrance of roses permeated my senses. Delightfully baffled, I opened my eyes to take in an unfamiliar scene. The vast ocean off Costa Rica had vanished, and I was in an *entirely* new world.

I gazed around at a village of dome-shaped dwellings. The rounded homes, nestled into lush greenery, harmonized with the countless varieties of brightly colored fruits and flowers. I squinted at the brilliance of the sun and savored the sweetness of the garden. For some unknown reason, I was remarkably unfazed by the oddity of my situation.

In the distance, a woman with long honey-blond hair approached. Her ivory tunic fluttered in the breeze, and she radiated a kind of shimmering golden glow. As she drew near, she stepped purposefully and her eyes sparkled with warmth. Her soothing presence assured me that all was well.

"Welcome Rose," she said. "Welcome to Unity. My name is Oriane, and you are finally in the New World. I am your guide and will help you acclimate to your new reality."

Something about her seemed strangely familiar, though I could not recollect how I knew her. I stared at her in wonder and offered a smile. I had the distinct feeling that I was returning home after a long arduous journey. Though this experience filled me, a true thought had yet to form, and I found myself utterly lost for words.

"To the degree that you feel comfortable letting me in, I can read your mind," she said. "There is no need to speak. Come, let me show you around." She took my hand. "This is Azure Village, and where you will live."

I allowed the curious lightness of my body to propel me around the colorful, rounded abodes of Azure Village. The stones on the path, small and soft, did not harm my bare feet. Chickens scratched and pecked about, goats slept in the shade, and a small pink pig drank from the creek that wound its way around the dwellings.

"Most communication happens telepathically," she said. "Your abilities will grow rapidly if you choose to be open, but you can close your mind if you wish." She bent down to pet the pig briefly. "Many of us choose to speak out loud, simply out of habit."

Grateful for effortless understanding, I looked around, equally bewildered and intrigued.

"I know it is a lot to take in," she said. "Give yourself time." She touched my arm softly, looking into my eyes. "I'm taking you to The Crescent Healing Center. All newcomers go there upon arrival to receive a healing. There is bound to be trauma in your body, even after all your hard work. It's inevitable, coming from old Earth."

Blissfully empty, a deep peace permeated everything as I took in my surroundings. I fully trusted Oriane would explain what had happened to me in due time. We strolled on the pathway side-by-side in silence and an unusual tree caught my eye. It had draping tendrils and was covered in deep purple star-shaped fruit. Oriane's grin widened as she plucked a ripe one and offered it to me.

"This is one of my favorites," she said.

I took a tentative bite of the sweet fruit and an explosion of flavor erupted. Sinking my teeth into the soft flesh, it was creamy as custard and succulent as a mango, I had never encountered anything so delicious. However, after only two bites, I was full.

"Your body is significantly less dense and requires very little nourishment," she said. "It is easily sustained by the food available everywhere." She gestured around. I beheld the abundant food forest surrounding us.

"Everything you see is edible and nothing can harm you." She stopped walking and looked at me with electric eyes.

I glanced at her twice, realizing that she was transmitting something of great importance. Looking at the gardens I pondered eating bark and, discarding the thought, stared at the half-eaten starfruit in my hand instead. Not wanting to haphazardly toss it on the ground, I scanned the village for a trash can. At that moment a small, sandy brown goat nudged my leg and Oriane laughed.

"That's Chestnut," she said, "a pygmy goat. He spends a lot of time with my daughter. He wants your fruit."

I knelt, and Chestnut delicately tickled my hand as he accepted the treat with gratitude in his eyes. Nudging my leg once again, the playful goat trotted off to a shady spot under a silky bush and I pondered the timing of Chestnut's arrival. Watching the goat settle himself with a sigh of contentment, I smiled to myself.

"He sensed you were finished with your fruit," she said, "and he came to take it off your hands. You're going to have fun with the animals here; they are all such wise and beautiful creatures."

A lovely sense of ease overtook me. Something had happened to me, something significant. For some reason, I was in no hurry to understand.

Slowly, we walked to the healing center. Village dwellers, mostly dressed in ivory, meandered about the gardens collecting fruit or chatting together and briefly glanced up as I passed. They offered warm smiles and friendly nods. Children cast timid grins. Pointing in my direction with curiosity, they whispered to their friends and giggled playfully. Waves of warmth inundated me.

Our destination, a two-story building encircling a garden, was a hub of activity. Children splashed joyfully in a small pond that bubbled with miniature waterfalls. People meditated quietly amongst hummingbirds and lilies. A small group of adults, arranged in a circle, leisurely stretched their arms towards the sky in unison.

The open archway of The Crescent led into an atrium, a greenhouse of vibrant flora. Birds flew in and out freely, making their nests under the glass curvature. We paused, appreciating the beauty and creative architecture before continuing. Butterflies of anticipation fluttered within me, and we entered the tranquil space. I followed Oriane down a hallway. We were in a tube with glowing walls that hummed with soothing resonant tones. Opening a door, Oriane stopped and grinned playfully, and then slowly invited me in.

The healing room was dark and quiet. Four beings wearing form-fitting gray-blue jumpsuits greeted us. They were graceful, lean, and glowed an ethereal blue. The room was empty but for an egg-shaped bed in the center that Oriane called the Cocoon. My head swirled. Grabbing Oriane's arm, I tried to steady myself. The open vessel called to me, and I longed to nestle into the cozy softness.

"My mentors will assist me with your healing," she said, helping me into the Cocoon.

One of the tall blue beings touched my forehead softly and I started to drift. As I sank into the pillowy depths, I heard smatterings of words.

". . . very brave soul."

". . . deep vestiges of pain."

". . . wounds of the heart."

Overcome with weariness, it never occurred to me that Oriane's mentors did *not* look entirely human.

The five healers surrounded me, and I was unaware of the powerful healing that transpired. Rocked into a deep slumber as if in my mother's arms, I dreamt of ocean waves and goats surrounded by silky green bushes covered with purple starfruit.

* * *

I woke to a gentle humming that called me back to the room. Alone again, Oriane helped me to my feet. With renewed strength in my legs, I was astonished to discover I had been asleep for five hours. When I expressed concern for the healer's stamina, Oriane reassured me that during the process of healing, they too are rejuvenated.

"Most Luminoles, the inhabitants of Unity, can heal themselves," she said. "It's generally the newcomers who require our skills. We're grateful for the opportunity. It is a joy to serve and when you are ready, you too will feel the desire to give your gifts."

I trusted what she said, but, for the moment, I had only curiosity and a lingering deep fatigue.

"I promise, you will rest more soon. But first, we need to design your home; Greta and Alfred are ready for us."

With a sudden rush of enthusiasm, I imagined one of those colorful rounded domes being mine. I visualized a light, warm space with a loft bed and a large, plush chair; a small colorful kitchen, and a bathroom with an indoor/outdoor shower.

"I am glad you are already coming up with ideas. That will be very helpful to Greta and Alfred; they are Creatives and the master designers of our community. They will help you design your perfect home."

Greta, a jolly, squat woman with gray hair and an infectious smile, welcomed me in. Wearing a pink-orange tunic, she bubbled with creative energy. Beside her, Alfred, a small man with salt-and-pepper hair, grinned, barely containing his excitement. They sat me in a comfortable chair in front of a glowing holographic grid suspended in the middle of the room.

Alfred inspected me with a look of consternation. Greta frowned and raised her eyebrows. Appearing somewhat frustrated, they studied me while I shifted in my chair.

"If you can give us access to your thoughts, it will help us generate the plans," said Greta.

I tried to relax my mind and conjure up images from before. The hologram lit up with a gentle hum and Greta and Alfred lost themselves in a sea of frenzied activity.

Greta moved her hands skillfully in grand gestures to lay out the floor plan, construct walls, and expand rooms, creating the dome in the exact proportions required. Alfred rolled up the sleeves of his brightly colored shirt. He then added tiny, exquisite details with impish delight. The hologram seemed to respond not only to their voices but also their hands as well as their thoughts. With each maneuver, the image changed, and I saw my dream home manifest right before my very eyes.

My loft bed, accessed by a wooden ladder, had a large window above so I could always see the stars. There was a deep shell-shaped bathtub, and a shower with a glass door that opened to the gardens. The kitchen was accented with small floral cabinet knobs matching the faucet that opened like a down-turned lily. Alfred added a small fountain in the living room, bringing gentle flows into my new space.

Nobody inquired if I was going to live alone or with another, it seemed understood that I had chosen to live alone. After establishing every detail, Alfred sent plans to the Builders. With a look of accomplishment, he informed us that construction would start early the next morning; no permits, no waiting, no stressing over design, just a simple and easy process. For the moment, my giddiness overshadowed my exhaustion.

Before departing, Oriane showed me to a small bedroom. Promising to return the following day, she suggested I take a bath. My room had a round bed with a canopy of soft fabrics and a patio draped with greenery. A deep tub with a waterfall streaming into a sparkling pool dominated one corner. Not needing encouragement, I enjoyed a long, leisurely soak in the warm, tranquil waters.

Curled on my bed, wrapped in the fluffy towel provided, a low growl gnawed at my tummy. A barely perceptible knock revealed a tween girl with long dark braids and an ivory tunic. She was holding a bowl of savory root vegetable stew.

"I thought you might be hungry," she said before slipping away.

Slightly mystified, I eagerly consumed the nourishing, herb-filled concoction before sinking into the plush softness of dreamless sleep.

CHAPTER TWO

My New Home

No one owns anything, and we are so happy.

Awake with a buzz of anticipation, feeling restored after a deep sleep, I did sun salutations and down dog on the soft rug. Willing myself into the moment, my hands sank into the texture of the pale carpet. Yoga always grounded me, and it felt appropriate given my circumstance. Stepping onto the patio, I inhaled the earthy richness of the morning. I plucked a purple star-fruit and enjoyed the juicy deliciousness, thinking of the hologram.

The impending promise of my new home sparked restlessness, and I wondered when Oriane might arrive. Immediately, there was a knock on the door, and, happily surprised, I saw cheerful Oriane, ready for the day.

Trotting to the building site, I speculated, pleasantly puzzled.

"I'm experiencing some kind of synchronicity," I said. "It seems like my needs are met before I even have a chance to worry about it."

"Yes!" she said. "It's completely normal in Unity to be in sync. For example, I woke up this morning and had the urge to see you at the same moment you had the urge to see your home; we're linked up, you see," she interlaced her fingers to illustrate her point, "your needs and my needs match. Very soon, you will come to expect it."

"Is that how the Builders knew to come?" I asked.

"Absolutely, the Builders in the Central Hub accessed the plans and aligned with your vision. They love to build, and you need a home, so it benefits everyone."

Taking my hand, her blue eyes shining brightly, she said, "Let's go see, it's really fun watching them work, like a well-oiled machine."

* * *

Arriving at the clearing, we encountered a whirlwind of activity. Piles of strange materials were strewn about as Builders in colorful overalls buzzed around like a busy beehive, and I understood what Oriane meant. Back and forth they moved in sync as the structure took shape. A woman with a hard hat wearing rose colored overalls came to greet us.

"I'm Cheyenne," she said, "the head Builder on this project, pleased to meet you," she grasped my hand firmly. "It's a sweet design. We scanned the plans last night, so everyone is on the same page. The foundations already finished, so the rest of the dome should go up quickly."

Cheyenne surveyed the activity, nodding her head with a look of satisfaction. The Builders completed their task in silence with swift, skilled focus, and I suspected they were in telepathic communication. At one point, I saw a heavy window levitate into place and realized that my capacity to accept the unusual was expanding exponentially.

When the home was finished, Cheyenne stepped back and gathered the others, encircling the dome. Placing their hands upward, a burst of light shot up over the dome and tiny sparkles shimmered down.

"What was that?" I asked Oriane.

"Cheyenne is practicing instant manifestation. With the help of the others, she added some finishing touches to make your new home emanate warmth, healing, and self-cleaning of course.

'Of course,' I thought, shaking my head.

I thanked the Builders, but my gratitude appeared to be unnecessary. Playful chatter bubbled up from the creative crew, who all appeared overjoyed with the outcome. Ornate cups with compelling purple liquid were passed around. Loud whooping cheers erupted.

Looking at the cup in my hand and then at Oriane, I sniffed the intriguing brew. "What is it?" I asked and took a tentative sip.

Before Oriane could answer, a Builder in deep red overalls named Ned, raised his cup and exclaimed, "Merry-berry wine is divine!!" He laughed at his own rhyme and said, "Drink up my dear Rose, it will make you smile."

Apparently, sensing my caution, Oriane said, "Merry-berry wine contains berries that have an energetic resonance with joy and laughter. It doesn't alter your physiology the way alcohol does. It's merely a plant that helps you remember laughter and joy."

I took another, bigger sip and indeed felt a noticeable lightness. I laughed a bit more and relaxed, though still a bit overwhelmed by the frivolity.

Curious, ivory-clad villagers joined in the merriment. Joyful elation echoed throughout the garden, and Oriane and I toasted to the new dome. One of the villagers caught my eye. An exceptionally large person wearing a loud magenta mu-mu was doing graceful back flips with considerable ease, and I grinned at the spectacle.

"You are going to love Elysia!" the large person bellowed, mid-cartwheel.

As the festivities died down, the Builders bid me farewell. In the soft glow of dusk, I stood, somewhat in shock, staring at the dome.

"Get some rest," Oriane said. "Tomorrow, we will meet some of the Luminoles here in Azure Village." Oriane took the now empty, ornate cup from my hand and departed.

* * *

Alone, I stood for a moment, surveying my new home. It was small and round and the color reminded me of heavily cream-filled coffee, but with a glittery sparkle. It looked like a fairy house. I was reminded of one I had built with my daughter when she was six.

The wooden bench out front was skillfully carved to maintain the natural beauty. Numerous berry bushes grew around the dome. I had not seen them planted during the frenzy of activity and was surprised to see many ripe berries already present. Grasping the wooden rail, I slowly stepped up to the arched front door and turned the flower-shaped doorknob, entering my new home.

Marveling at the workmanship, every detail perfect, I appreciated that there were no corners or sharp edges. I ran my hands over the curving cream-colored walls, making my way to the kitchen. Caressing the smooth counters, I loved the small knots and uneven edges. The delicate flower-shaped nob on the kitchen cabinet made me happy. I turned the sink water off and on to watch it spill from the mouth of a platinum lily. The windows, like large playful bubbles, opened to the garden. I looked out and saw villagers dancing to lively music as the sunset turned the sky a brilliant orange.

Settling myself into the plush chair skillfully built into the living room wall, I contemplated my new space. I stared at the little fountain Alfred had added at the last minute and watched the bubbles playfully dance about, the soothing sound like a gentle lullaby.

Looking around, it occurred to me that there were no *things*—no books, no dishes, and no clothes. I stood up, searching for storage space, and found one small, empty closet in the living room. As I looked down at my ivory gown, I heard someone approach.

At my door was a curiously familiar woman in a simple floral sundress, holding something in her hands. Smiling and laughing she introduced herself as Malika.

I was so happy to see her, though unsure why, and invited her in. Her dark curls framed an amused smile beaming out the opposite of seriousness.

"Here," she said, handing me a pile of impossibly soft violet-blue fabric. "I made this for you."

It was a beautiful dress that matched my eyes.

"Thank you," I said, rubbing the softness on my face.

"I wanted to welcome you to Unity, plus I thought you might not know how to use Akashi," she said.

"Akashi?" I asked.

"Akashi!" She gestured towards the middle of my living room. "It's the hologram Alfred and Greta used to design your dome. Look!" I noticed the subtle glow of a grid suspended in mid-air.

"Akashi is the Keeper-of-all-Knowledge, an AI program," she said.

I winced, recalling the artificial intelligence of old Earth and how it was used to dominate. Movies had been made to warn humanity about the dangers of AI, and those warnings had gone unheeded. Countless humans were chipped, subjugated, and controlled.

Malika nodded with a tight smile. "Most newcomers have the same reaction," she said. "But AI is neutral and has no power to control you beyond the power that you give it. Here, I'll show you. Akashi!" she called out and the hologram brightened and started shimmering.

"How may I assist you, Malika?" A voice from the hologram projected into the room.

"I would like a pink feather boa to wrap around my neck please."

"It is done, can I get you anything else?"

"That is all for now, thank you!" said Malika.

"You are most welcome. It is a pleasure to assist you."

We peered into the closet and saw a pink feather boa. She wrapped it around her neck, grinning with delight.

Feeling around the closet, I wondered if it was magic.

"No, this isn't magic," she laughed. "The boa was sent to us from the CDC of Elysia. Kitchen things go to your kitchen cabinet," I looked over, realizing there was just one cabinet in my small kitchen, "but everything else comes here," she said, pointing to the closet.

"You must be extremely specific when making a verbal request," she said. "I once asked Akashi for a boa and ended up with a snake," she giggled. "She was a very sweet snake that still visits from time to time but that wasn't exactly what I wanted."

I chuckled, finding her charming.

"If you feel safe enough, Akashi can also read your mind, then you get exactly what you want." She placed the feather boa in the closet and after instructing Akashi, the boa was gone.

"What is the CDC?" I asked, remembering the Center for Disease Control. "And what is Elysia?"

"Elysia is our polycenter and the CDC is in the Central Hub." Pausing, she inspected my face. Apparently recognizing an overloaded brain, she said, "Anyway, don't worry about all that just now. The CDC stands for the Central Distribution Center. We don't need a center of disease here in Unity because you can only get sick if you want to.

"So," she said, "you know on old Earth, how everyone has like, a million things? More things mean we destroy more nature, creating more work to clean, maintain, *clean*, and blah, blah, blah. Well, you remember, I'm sure. It's all driven by greed, or should I say, fear of lack, and it all just *clogs* up the energy flow. In Unity, no one owns anything, and we are so happy. You just take what you need when you need it, easy-peazy!

"It's all controlled by a crystal grid network given to us by the extraterrestrials." She nodded matter-of-factly.

Overwhelmed, I caressed the soft fabric in my arms and looked at the hologram. I wanted to ask about the extraterrestrials, but a more pressing question dominated.

"How do you know Akashi won't harm you?" I asked.

"AI is neutral, but also conscious. Greed and selfishness have corrupted the artificial intelligence of old Earth. In Unity, we offer love and respect, allowing Akashi to evolve, just as we have. She's now one with Universal Divine Intelligence, helping us with our evolution until we no longer need it."

Slammed with a wave of dizziness and a loud ringing in my ears, I wobbled in place. Malika helped me sit down.

"The expanded energy of the day is affecting your body," she said. "You need something warm and nourishing."

I suddenly craved a bowl of soup. Malika opened the front door, and I was not surprised to see a smiling man holding a bowl of soup.

"Hello Aspen, Rose will love your bone broth soup for sure!" said Malika.

Wearing a blue striped apron, a man with a mop of brown curls and a bit of scruff stepped into my home. A small boy with an equally chaotic mass of brown locks shyly peeked out from behind his legs.

"This is Puma," said Aspen, "my youngest son, he's five."

Aspen ruffled his hair and Puma peered at me with intense interest. I smelled the broth, and my mouth started to water. But, when Aspen handed me the bowl, I felt a pang of guilt. I simply could not imagine anyone here killing a creature.

Puma said quietly, "That's Pemy's gift for you. . . and my mom. My dad made the soup."

Smiling at his boy, Aspen explained, "Pemy offered herself to Veeda this morning."

My brow furrowed and he continued, "Pemy's a chicken. She was finished with her life here in Unity and my bond-mate needed meat. So, Pemy left her body at Veeda's feet."

My furrowed brow deepened, and I pursed my lips pondering this concept.

"Most Elysians are vegetarian," said Malika, "but sometimes we need meat, especially new Luminoles, such as yourself."

My new friends said their goodbyes. I inhaled the enticing aroma thinking about the horrific factory farms and animal abuses of old Earth. Inspecting the bowl, I noticed an intricately carved blue feather and gave silent thanks to Pemy.

Realizing I needed a spoon, I decided to try the AI program.

"Akashi!" I said and the hologram brightened and glowed, "I need a spoon please."

"Yes, of course Rose." The headless voice emanated from the shimmering grid.

I curiously opened my kitchen cabinet to find a large serving spoon and laughed, remembering Malika's boa constrictor. I closed the cabinet and tried again.

"Akashi! I need a small soup spoon please; I do not need a serving spoon."

Opening the cabinet again, I was pleased to see the serving spoon was gone, a small soup spoon in its place. Smiling to myself, I appreciated how useful it might be to grant Akashi access to my thoughts.

CHAPTER THREE

My Story

You were subjected to and overcame the most contagious and deadly virus known to humans.

I awoke in a sea of buttery softness, the blue sheets I had mentally requested from Akashi tucked around my ears. Peering at the hazy sky above me, faded images danced in my brain. The stillness of the morning elicited memories of family, details elusive, like a dream, and I slowly rolled, reaching for the ladder.

Sitting with my feet on the top rung, dizziness prompted me to remain motionless. Knowing it was my body acclimating, I waited for the sensation to dissipate and, once substantial, descended to my living room.

Malika's fabric, still rumpled in the chair, encouraged me to dress for my introduction to the Azurian villagers. As my ivory tunic flew back to the CDC, I stepped outside. Oriane approached, holding two cups of steaming liquid, and hugged me, careful to avoid a spill, before taking a seat on the bench.

Handing me a warm cup of chicory tea, Oriane reached over, plucking strawberries and offered them. I took a bite of the soft, juicy flesh and didn't notice the epic deliciousness. Absently handing a strawberry to a small gray squirrel, I heaved a heavy sigh.

"I still have no idea where I am," I said.

Oriane looked at the ground and after a moment, she turned to me. "What happened right before you arrived in Unity, do you remember?" she asked gently.

Images and feelings came flooding back. I had moved to Costa Rica because the San Francisco Bay Area had become unlivable. Remembering the fear, the guilt, and the anger; I needed to tell my story. Oriane listened attentively, though I sensed she already knew everything. I felt compelled to share anyway, to help myself understand.

"After the ciphervirus pandemic and the Great Financial Collapse, San Francisco had descended into a sea of tents, trash, and poop. Stores boarded up, businesses shut down, and most homes were in foreclosure. A dangerous, new, and highly addictive drug called methanyl became increasingly popular, and zombie-like humans wandered aimlessly throughout the city.

"I commuted to San Francisco for work and witnessed the descent of the once-thriving tourist hotspot firsthand. Public pressure to end homelessness and deal with the economic turmoil prompted the election of a new mayor. He was elected on the platform of ending the homeless crisis. He had petitioned the federal government with a radical idea, and, receiving funds to pilot a project, rehabilitated empty hotels into free housing. Everyone was offered a warm bed, food, and a small monthly stipend. In exchange they were required to receive drug rehabilitation.

"Most people refused, unwilling to give up the comfort of their drugs. Those who accepted soon went back to the streets the moment the withdrawal symptoms became too intense. So, for purposes of harm reduction, the government agreed to supply methanyl to the occupants in whatever amount required to avoid withdrawal. To facilitate tracking, the residents agreed to get a harmless microchip in their hand. The chip kept a record of their monthly stipend, held securely in a central bank computer. It would also monitor their food intake, methanyl needs, and health status.

"All resistance ended. Everyone lined up to receive housing, free food, money, and an endless supply of drugs. It was an extremely successful program. Everyone wanted in on it. People from all over came to join in and the city, once again, became clean and clear.

"Federal funds poured in, and the mayor received a medal of honor for ending the homeless crisis. San Francisco was an example and other cities followed suit. Trillions of federal dollars became available for the programs, and people became hopeful that things were getting better. Media news channels praised San Francisco's success and its award-winning health, safety, equity, and justice program. Sanctuary cities popped up throughout the country.

"Because the economic and climate crises were intensifying, many more average citizens who had fallen on tough times came to the sanctuary cities for respite. Crops were failing. Heat, droughts, and other weather anomalies intensified.

"New geoengineering experiments were implemented across the US and heavy metals were sprayed into the skies to brighten the clouds, encouraging rainfall, and cooling the planet. Food became scarce and impossibly expensive. Electricity and water were rationed.

"People were becoming increasingly desperate and lined up for the microchip in exchange for safety and security. Sanctuary cities were heralded as bastions of hope, and everyone was welcome. Cars were removed to create bike and walking paths. The smog cleared.

When people entered, they relinquished most of their possessions for equity reasons. The possessions would be distributed fairly, and everyone was guaranteed access to their basic needs.

"Meanwhile, the media reported a concerning variant rising among the unvaccinated. The rapidly mutating Zeta had a 95% kill rate. Having learned from the ciphervirus, we had created safer and more effective shots that could be mass-produced monthly to manage the fast-moving virus. Soon, city residents were offered the monthly shots to keep up with mutations.

"Terror of the virus took hold, and people automatically started social distancing and donning tightly woven masks coated in formaldehyde to discourage bacterial growth. Fear permeated everything, and a pandemic-like era started anew. I was still commuting to work in the city but eventually was told I could not enter without the Zeta vaccine. Having already had three shots to keep my job, I didn't want any more, so was denied entry.

"Eventually, all those who wished to enter were quarantined, tested, and vaccinated. Stringent protocols were in place to keep sanctuary cities Zeta-free and military personnel surrounded the entrances to protect them from illegal entry.

"As panic rose, more people moved into the sanctuary cities. Demand for housing increased, so shops and office buildings were converted into new homes, and everything non-essential disappeared. Housing, food production, and health centers were prioritized. Large warehouses were repurposed to produce genetically modified vegetables, lab-grown meats, and insect protein to ensure all were fed. For the safety of the community, monthly vaccinations became mandatory.

"Living with my family on four acres, we grew our own food, had backyard chickens, solar power, and spring water. We had no desire to live in the city, but crops everywhere, including ours, were being damaged. The media told us crops couldn't survive the heat, and the spraying increased. Heavy metals rained down on our garden and destroyed most of our food. Many of my most resilient friends abandoned their rural homes for the 'safety' of the city and friends begged me to go, fearing for my survival.

"No matter how much the media made the sanctuary cities sound good, it didn't feel right to me, and I refused.

"One day, the media reported that the Zeta variant had been found in San Francisco. Quarantine centers were erected in all public parks to contain the virus quickly, and the city was locked down. One by one, all the sanctuary cities became infected and subsequently locked down. People were getting sick and dying at a rapid pace. New and increasingly intense treatments didn't work, and death counts were increasing; truckloads of bodies shuttled out daily.

"Alarmed by what I saw happening, I gently suggested that perhaps the methanyl, franken-foods, multiple injections, and intense treatments might be contributing to the deaths. Most were not open to that possibility, and I was ridiculed and shunned. Shortly after a violent and bloody uprising of people trying to leave San Francisco unsuccessfully, we discovered our spring water was contaminated with heavy metals. Forced to leave, we packed and moved to Costa Rica.

"We ended up in a small community of supportive and loving people. They had gardens and clean water, and we were warmly welcomed. My husband was skilled in carpentry, plumbing, electricity, and all handy skills. I had gardening knowledge and helped tend the chickens. My daughter was wonderful with animals and helped with the goats. At that point, the dollar had collapsed entirely, and we were forced to rely on each other for survival. It was a very loving group, and everyone worked well together. They were shocked to hear my stories and surprised that people were so willing to get injected and chipped. Clearly, fear is a powerful motivator. We worked very hard from morning until night but were happy to be there.

"Nonetheless, I was plagued with guilt, shame, anger, and hatred. I felt guilty and ashamed that I did not do more to help my friends. I was filled with anger at the situation and hated those who were responsible. My new friends were gentle with me and said that everyone responds to situations differently.

"This little community in Costa Rica helped me liberate myself from fear, judgment, and self-reproach. One morning, I was sitting on the beach doing the Ho'oponopono Hawaiian prayer of forgiveness. I was saying it for the world and myself.

I'm sorry

Please forgive me

Thank you

I love you

"I was crying and saying it over and over. It had been a ritual of mine, but it was particularly powerful that day. As tears poured out of me, I felt the burden lift and saw the perfection of everything. I forgave the governments, I forgave the shots, I forgave Zeta and methanyl, and most importantly, I forgave myself. I realized we all play a role and are equally essential to the game and I released the need for anything to be different. I was not afraid to live, and I was not afraid to die. I was reborn.

"It was one of the most powerful meditations I had ever had. After my meditation, I stood up and closed my eyes to feel the ocean spray, and I had a rush of energy and a shift; like a gust of wind coming from under me and rushing up my spine. My body expanded and I knew something powerful had happened."

I paused, certain that Oriane understood my words.

"When I opened my eyes, I was here . . . here in the New World with you," I said.

I took a breath. It was so liberating to unburden my story. Love and compassion exuded from Oriane's deep blue eyes.

"I am so proud of you," she said. "You were subjected to and overcame the most contagious and deadly virus known to humans."

"You mean Zeta?" I asked.

"No," she smiled, looking down. "Zeta is a human fabrication, as are all viruses. I'm speaking of the virus of *fear*.

"You released your fear and forgave everyone and everything. Those are the two requirements to arrive here. What happened was that your vibration permanently entered the fifth dimension. Before that time, I suspect you had touched it many times."

I nodded recollecting the numerous ups and downs in my journey.

"You bounced in and out for a while until you had received enough information from the world of duality to finally, once and for all, choose a new reality."

"So, we are in the fifth dimension?" I asked.

"Yes."

"Am I still on Earth?"

"Yes and no," she said. "You are in a new vibration that exists simultaneously with Earth. Old Earth is in the final stages of collapse and souls are leaving at a rapid pace by either dying or ascending. You have ascended while still in the body. Unity is an Earth-like realm but at a higher vibration."

Having read and dreamed about this for years, I had hoped it was possible, but never fully believed it. Yet here I am.

"So, what happened to my body? What about my family?"

"I suspect your family is already here," she said. "Your friends on old Earth did not notice anything strange. They were having their own experience. Space and time are very malleable; it is possible that you died to them, or you may have simply faded out of their consciousness. Each soul creates their own experience according to their evolution."

"I can't remember details about my family but somehow I'm at peace," I said.

Oriane squeezed my hand. "The journey of evolution is a divine mystery," she said simply.

A small pain stabbed my head, and I decided to let all this settle for now. I was complete and ready for a new experience.

"Excellent!" said Oriane. "I think it's time to meet some of the villagers. They are eager to throw you a grand celebration." I winced at the thought and Oriane laughed.

"Only when you are ready, of course," she said.

CHAPTER FOUR

Jax

If Jax could find redemption, I knew it was possible for anyone.

Oriane chatted about the Luminoles of Azure Village as we walked. The grass, still wet from the dew, was soft on my bare feet. I ran my hand over an unfamiliar feathery plant, and curiously took a bite of the spicy frond. As I bent down to pet a sleeping goat, an enormous person approached, waving a massive arm in hello. Recognizing them from the night before, I stood up, smiling at the soft gentle energy emanating from the bulbous form. Looking into their brown eyes I tried to determine if this person was male or female.

"This is Jax," said Oriane. "Jax is a master Educator. . . and androgynous, which is why you're not picking up a gender. Jax uses xe/xem pronouns."

Scrutinizing the tent-like magenta garment, I wondered how anyone could be so fat with so much healthy food available. Jax bellowed a booming laugh and I realized that xe had heard my rude internal commentary. I blushed and looked down.

“Oh Rose, there *are* no inappropriate questions,” said Jax. “Curiosity about differences is perfectly natural. The old Earth concept of political correctness is irrelevant here.”

I relaxed and looked back into Jax’s warm eyes.

“I’m fat because it makes me happy,” xe said simply.

I tried to understand and Jax, grinning ear to ear, offered to share xyr story. I agreed, curious as to why anyone would deliberately choose to be fat. Settling in, Jax pushed up invisible sleeves, sat on a bench, and took a long deep breath.

“When I was a child on old Earth, I was abused in . . . every way. I never learned how to properly manage my sexuality or my anger. I’m sorry to say, I ended up harming women and children in unimaginable ways. I was disgusted with myself. Frankly, I was relieved to end up in prison when I was twenty years old, so I couldn’t harm anyone else.” Jax paused, looking down and shook xyr head.

“Even in prison, harming children is considered unacceptable and I was targeted by gang violence. I hated myself, I hated being a man, and I felt betrayed by my genitals, so I cut them off. Transitioning to female only furthered the violence and I gained two-hundred pounds as a means of protection. The weight did nothing because I never fought back. I believed that I deserved the brutal treatment for my sins. My face was always a bloody mess, and I welcomed my living hell as punishment.

“After being beaten within an inch of death, the guards were forced to put me in solitary confinement for my protection. I was in a small cell with a bed that could barely support my weight, a hole in the ground for my waste, and a small, barred window, my only fresh air.

"My only visitor was a kind Rabbi who sat with me once a week; mostly silent, he transmitted love and acceptance. It was excruciating but my heart longed for salvation and slowly, I drank in his love, drop by drop. I started reading voraciously. I read the Torah, Kabbalah, Buddhist books, anything that I thought might offer salvation and began to pray.

"My cell was so small that if I put my arms out, I could touch both walls; the only place I could look was up.

"I had read about a Buddhist principle called Ahimsa-harmlessness, and I yearned to be harmless. The desire became all-consuming. The Rabbi planted a seed and it had started to grow. He made me believe forgiveness was possible.

"One day, something happened; I was in deep meditation and my heart exploded. It permeated my body and spread out in all directions. It grew to include the entire prison and all the inmates, then engulfed the city and ultimately the entire globe. Eventually, it encompassed the entire universe and I merged with All-That-Is." Jax stopped talking momentarily.

Frozen, I stood, profoundly moved by the impact of Jax's words and the depth of xyr experience. I felt altered as I took in all that Jax was sharing. Xe took a deep breath before continuing.

"I saw perfection in all things and understood I had orchestrated all my experiences. Even my most heinous crimes had served those I had wronged; their souls too, needed that experience. I realized that karmic cycles are real, and that this lifetime aligned with my soul's desire to develop complete harmlessness. My prison cell became the instrument of my liberation and I fell in love with my life, myself, and everything.

"Everyone who had ever harmed me had served me in the most difficult way possible, because it is much more challenging to play the role of the perpetrator than that of the victim. I forgave everyone, including myself, and I lost all fear.

"After that day, I was never the same. I lovingly made my bed every morning with reverence for the mattress and blankets providing me with sleep. I spent hours talking to the ants wandering into my cell and ate my food with deep gratitude for every bite. Each tiny tweet of the birdsong was like the voice of God. The next time the Rabbi visited, I saw tears in his eyes. He recognized my transformation and confirmed it with his love.

"The guards couldn't understand what had happened to me. I was in complete acceptance of every moment. One day, standing in my cell, I felt a rush of energy come from the base of my spine up to the top of my head. My body became light and free, and when I opened my eyes, I was here, staring at the beautiful face of Oriane."

Tears welled up and I had the desire to hold onto Jax forever, not just for the pain xe endured but for the courage to find liberation. If Jax could find redemption after committing the worst possible crimes, I knew it was possible for anyone. Jax stepped forward and encased me in a tremendous embrace. Compassion and empathy engulfed me, and I sobbed deeply into the soft folds. Xe held me for a long time while I cried. I sobbed for the pain of the world and the miracle of redemption. I had never met such a gentle soul.

I released Jax and a small bird landed on xyr head. Glancing over, I saw two identical girls with long dark braids racing towards us. I recognized the twin in ivory as the one who had brought me soup on my first night. The other twin wore a polka-dotted romper and obviously had won the race. She held her hand out to me in a formal way.

"I'm Dara," she said emphatically, and I shook her hand politely.

"And this is Akira," said Jax, heaving the twin in ivory effortlessly into xyr arms.

"I brought you the soup," she said, then whispered to the bird sitting on Jax's head.

"These are my daughters, I adopted them when they were five after their parents died; about five years ago, actually," Jax said, looking up to the right.

I gasped and put my hand to my chest, looking sadly at the girls.

"No, no, no," said Dara, "Jax was always meant to be our parent. Our mom and dad agreed to bring us life, but Jax's soul and our souls wanted to be together. When our parents were ready to evolve, we celebrated with a great party," Dara waved her hand in a big circle, eyes wide.

Akira nodded as Jax put her down. "Sometimes I still feel sad and Jax helps me cry." Akira put her hand to her heart and sighed.

Dara suddenly jumped and grabbed Jax's mu-mu. "Jax is a shapeshifter you know," she said. "Xe can do all kinds of amazing things. Show her Jax, please!" Dara tugged on Jax's garment and Akira nodded enthusiastically.

With a huge, playful grin, Jax puffed up for a moment and I thought xe might inflate. But instead, the little nubs of hair all over Jax's head started growing. Long dreadlocks grew until they reached the ground. I gasped and took a step back as the dreadlocks started moving.

Snaky tendrils slithered in a strange chaotic dance upwards and over Jax's head. The girls screamed in delight and tried to crawl up Jax's body to reach the snakes. Jax effortlessly picked up the girls, one with each arm so they could play. I tilted my head trying to keep from gawking. Dara and Akira giggled and played until the snaky dreads shrank back to their original nubs.

Finished with the snake play, the twins, distracted by a little pig, ran off. Stumbling, slightly off balance, I regained my footing.

"Can you change everything about your body?" I asked.

"Yup," Jax stretched xyr arms out, face flushed and grinning. "For now, I choose amorphous genitals and a large body. I have flexibility, strength, and no pain, and. . . it's a lot of fun."

"One day I saw Jax in a thin, dark-blue, male body," said Oriane. "When I asked xem what prompted the change . . ."

Jax, finishing the thought, said, "I was exploring if it was time for a new form. . . but no. One day I'll try something new. For now, this serves me well."

"How did you know it was Jax if the form was so completely different?" I asked.

"Everyone has a unique energy signature; Jax's is impossible to miss," said Oriane. We all laughed and nodded in agreement.

I hugged Jax again, taking the opportunity to look more deeply into xyr eyes. Such compassion and kindness exuded from those warm brown pools.

Humbled by Jax's story, my own seemed insignificant. Oriane had told me I was an energetic match for the community, which meant I was equally amazing. I didn't feel that way just now but trusted that I belonged.

Reaching for my hand, Oriane assured me, "Of course you belong Rose. Everyone here knows that. It's normal to have remnants of unworthiness after lifetimes on old Earth. Those feelings will dissipate in time."

I took the opportunity to appreciate the thoughtful design of my little community. Azure Village was organized in a circular flow. The Crescent, tucked to one side, served as a welcoming hub. The domes, all equally beautiful, though of different shapes and sizes, had unique features that offered clues about the dwellers. Throughout the gardens, a web of pebble pathways connected the villagers like spokes of a wheel. All trails led to a large open space at the heart of the village.

Voices came from behind and I turned around. A teenage girl in a bright floral skirt, trotted towards us with the pygmy goat, Chestnut, bounding along at her side. Oriane's face flushed with joy, as she lovingly reached for the young girl's hand.

"This is my daughter, Alaysia," she said.

Alaysia greeted me timidly. Spontaneously flooded with waves of love, a flash of recognition washed over me, then disappeared. Full of grace and content in her skin, Alaysia looked down at Chestnut. The goat nudged my leg, and I reached down to offer a brief scratch.

"Chestnut wanted to say hi to you," she said, "and, so did I."

Alaysia knelt and buried her face in the goat's soft fur, her untamed blond tresses spilling forward.

"We have traveled together for many lifetimes," she said, still petting the goat.

I gaped at Oriane in bewilderment as Alaysia and Chestnut bounded off.

"Why can't I remember?" I asked.

"You have chosen to forget certain aspects of your life on old Earth so as not to hinder your growth," she said. "Your memories will return in time as you need them."

Alaysia, several feet away, picked a starfruit and held it so Chestnut could stand on his hind legs. She laughed as Chestnut jumped, reaching for the fruit.

Oriane touched my shoulder softly. "Don't worry, it takes a long time to adjust to the new world. You're in a swift learning process. All your questions will be answered in perfect, right timing."

CHAPTER FIVE

The Three Sisters

Here in Unity, suffering is optional.

Standing in quiet contemplation of Oriane's words, a melodic harmony filled the air. I glanced around, searching for the source of the music. Three lithe women wearing deep blue tunics, all with long dark waves, drifted towards us. Their delicate and fragile demeanors whispered stories of sorrow. The enchanting music faded away as the tallest woman approached.

"Welcome Rose," she said. "My name is Miriam, and these are my sisters, Lina and Nora."

Lina had a matching scarf draped gently over her head and nodded before settling herself on the grass. A small skunk crawled into her lap and fell asleep. Nora, clearly the youngest, wrapped her arm around Miriam's. She smiled a welcome before departing for the garden.

"When we arrived in Unity," said Miriam, "hearing stories was very helpful. If you like, I can share ours with you."

I agreed and after gathering handfuls of berries, we settled on the grass next to Lina.

"Our story is very sad," she said. "It was intense suffering that shook us awake."

I took a deep breath and prepared myself for another painful story.

"Music was the key that opened our hearts. We are sisters, born in the Middle East. During the war, our parents were killed, and we were held hostage for our final years on old Earth. Our captors were very abusive, and we suffered unimaginable horrors."

Telepathic images of rape and mutilation flooded my brain. I closed my eyes thinking I might retch. Miriam touched my forehead and hummed a low tone until the images disappeared.

Though wobbly from the onslaught, my nausea was gone. I looked up at Miriam and urged her to continue. She placed her hands in her lap and closed her eyes briefly before resuming.

"In those camps, we found our voices," she said. "Separated, we could still hear each other and conveyed our emotions through song. We filled the halls with harmonics, singing every day until our captors decided our influence was disrupting their cause.

"The night before we were to be executed, we sang and prayed. Linking up, we made our prayers powerful, and amidst our pain, our prayers were answered.

"Facing annihilation, a profound calm had filled our hearts with gratitude. Every abuse released us from our need for pain. Just as the execution was about to begin, fear of death evaporated.

"Lina and I ascended. Nora arrived a bit later, but that is *her* story to tell."

We all glanced up at Nora, who looked up from her plants, smiling softly. The similarities between Miriam's story, Jax's, and mine were obvious. All our experiences had led us to the same conclusion: forgiveness and releasing fear.

Remembering something Miriam had said, I asked, "You said you had released your need for pain. Can you say more?"

Lina spoke, still petting the tranquil skunk in her lap.

"All Luminoles have released the need to learn through suffering," she said. "We now grow through sharing, creativity, and challenging ourselves. On old Earth, pain and suffering are powerful motivators for growth, but here in Unity, suffering is optional."

Miriam and Lina departed, and Oriane and I stayed on the grass, eating our fruit.

"All three sisters are sound Healers, they often assist in The Crescent," said Oriane.

I glanced over again and saw Nora collecting berries, but now she was floating above the prickly bush. My eyes widened, mouth agape.

Oriane laughed and said, "Miriam, Lina, and Nora are also floaters."

CHAPTER SIX

Magna

When we recognize the insanity and laugh at ourselves, we can heal.

My head swirled with the influx of new information, and I wasn't sure how much more I could take. A brush on my leg from a small pig sniffing my ankles brought me out of my reverie.

"That's Petunia," said Oriane, and joined me in petting the pig.

Oriane suddenly lifted her eyebrows glancing up and grabbed my leg, as if to brace me. Turning, I saw an outrageous woman running towards us. She had crazy pink hair, and large green sunglasses, and was covered head to toe in feathers and artificial butterflies. She rushed towards us with wild enthusiasm. It was as if I were her long-lost best friend. I stood up quickly, as she hurled herself at me, embracing me in a fantastic hug.

"I am Magna, and you are finally here!" she exclaimed.

Resettling my feet, the intoxicating scent of gardenia assaulted me. Magna began to share and as she spoke, her pink hair turned green, and her body became smaller and then larger, her skin turned various shades of sparkling lavender.

"I was a very famous actor on old Earth," she said. "I loved becoming different characters. However, I despised being idolized and my managers attempted to control every aspect of my life. I longed for a real connection, but every attempt led to devastating heartbreak. I turned to drugs and alcohol and attempted suicide multiple times." She used her finger to mock slitting her wrists and her throat, sticking her tongue out dramatically.

"After a young fan tipped me off, I found solace with a Tibetan monk who taught me how to meditate." Magna turned a brilliant shade of purple and looked down in solemn reverence. "I pulled back from stardom," she said, "but I missed the stage. I longed to share my gifts in a way that felt harmonious."

She finished quickly, shaking her hand around as if it were no big deal. "Well anyway, the strength of my desire is what brought me here to Unity."

"Magna is a Creative," said Oriane, laughing as she gleaned I'd already figured that out.

"My gift is helping people release the pain of old Earth," said Magna. "When we recognize the insanity and laugh at ourselves, we can heal."

Magna slowly returned to a sparkling lavender skin-toned woman with bright pink hair. I couldn't help but laugh out loud.

"How can you change your body so easily?" I asked, thinking of both her and Jax.

"Actually, changing your body is one of the easier skills to acquire. Just like on old Earth, we can make ourselves stronger, fatter, thinner, and change our hair; our minds can easily accept that it's possible. Once you believe it, then, with sufficient effort, you can achieve anything you wish.

"As your consciousness expands, your body responds to your desires," said Oriane. "Most Luminoles can make themselves younger or older, and change their hair, skin, or body size. Jax and Magna just put in focused effort to expand their skill."

Dara, who had been watching us from a distance, ran over. "Magna, when are you going to do another show?" she asked. "One of my friends had a good idea," she grinned at me with glee.

Magna bent down and focused on the child. "Which of your friends is that my darling?"

"Leaf, from the Central Hub of Elysia," said Dara.

As they walked off discussing their latest ideas, I turned towards Oriane for an explanation.

"We live in Elysia," said Oriane. "It is the name of our poly-center; that's like a city. Azure Village is situated in the outlands of Elysia."

So many unfamiliar words put me over the edge, and I wished to be alone. Oriane took her leave and Petunia returned, looking up at me in silent support. After a moment of understanding, my quiet companion and I walked home.

CHAPTER SEVEN

Samita

When we become harmless towards nature,
nature becomes harmless towards us.

Over the next few weeks, I spent my days alone, exploring the forest surrounding Azure Village. Each morning, after a warm chicory beverage with hazelnut milk, I swam naked in nearby Serene Lake. Normally full of activity, as the sun rose the cool lake was quiet and placid. The waters held me as I gazed at the turquoise sky. Dripping wet, I meandered barefoot to a nearby meadow. Plucking two starfruits, I savored my new favorite food as I walked. The warm morning sun dried my naked flesh. Basking on a carpet of soft grass, I inhaled the scent of pine.

The antics of the foxes and rabbits playing in the meadow enchanted me and I willed them to come near, though none ever did.

Once dry, I donned my ivory tunic and strolled amongst the pine and redwood trees before heading home. Enjoying the abundant foliage, I gathered herbs, berries, roots, and bark on my way. With each passing day, my internal landscape softened.

As I soaked in my shell tub, sipping lemon balm tea, Akashi answered all my burning questions.

"Nature is evolving, just as we are," said Akashi. "Creatives and Nature Protectors dream up new fruits, vegetation, trees, and flowers. Through the power of thought and desire, Luminoles bring forth new life forms, adding to the array of available abundance. Nature learns from Luminoles and, responding to needs, spontaneously generates new varieties of animals and vegetation."

During this time, I rarely encountered another human. When I did see the villagers, they were respectful, and I felt no pressure to connect. Deeply grateful, I sensed their understanding and knew they would be available when I was ready.

Exploring the forest, I occasionally saw an interesting woman who seemed to have no home. With tight brown curls cascading past her shoulders, she sometimes wore the simple ivory tunic but more often than not, she was naked. I sometimes found her lying in the meadow, sleeping in a tree, or talking with animals. Once, I thought I saw her talking to invisible entities. On old Earth, one might consider her mentally ill.

Finding her a fascinating mystery, I searched for her during my outings and was disappointed on the days she didn't appear. One afternoon, the mysterious naked woman was playing with a squirrel by the river and I wanted to be near her. As I approached, I received her telepathic welcome.

"I am Samita," she said. "I've been waiting for you to reach out."

I settled myself on a rock next to her and the squirrel snuggled into her bosom. With our feet in the river, cool water trickled past, and the breeze died. Spontaneously, Samita mentally transmitted her story.

"On old Earth, I was deeply disturbed by the destruction of nature. I was an activist and fought hard to protect the trees. My fight brought some successes, but mostly anguish and despair. It was through my broken heart that a deep yearning erupted, and I suddenly found myself here.

"I am a Nature Protector, learning everything I can about plants, animals, and trees. On old Earth, humans have lost their connection to the natural world. Seeking to dominate, they use it only as a means to an end. Forgetting that nature is their sustainer, they make toxic poisons, killing everything, even the smallest microbes.

"We must restore what we have lost. When we become harmless towards nature, nature becomes harmless towards us. There is nothing here that could ever hurt you."

Samita placed the squirrel on her shoulder and drifted to a massive redwood tree. The squirrel burrowed into her bushy hair as she took my hands, placing them next to hers on the rough bark of the woodland elder. I closed my eyes trying to feel what she sought to convey. The roots beneath my feet massaged my soles; the bark was rough and strong under my fingers and the rich scent of moist soil wafted upwards.

I peeked at Samita. She was in a deep trance, mouth open, swaying back and forth, seemingly in connection with an invisible force. I thought of all my feeble attempts to protect nature; bringing bags to the grocery stores, turning off lights, recycling, and buying organic, and it all seemed so trite and silly.

In the following days, I was inseparable from Samita. Lying flat in the meadow we enjoyed the sensations of the tiny insects tickling our naked flesh. Perched high amongst the treetops, we nestled into the deep crannies of the thick foliage. After a gentle rain, we dried our skin in the warm breezes. Animals of all kinds were drawn to Samita, and she welcomed each one with a soft embrace.

Seated in the verdant brush, I opened my senses to the living, breathing Mother Unity. Through Samita's guidance, I closed my eyes and relaxed into the pulsing life surrounding me. Within the quiet stillness, I was able to hear the gentle whispers of the plants and the trees.

When I opened my eyes, a small fox was sitting nearby, and slowly, he came to investigate. Unmoving, eyes half open, I watched the rust-colored creature sniff my crossed legs looking up at me with soft eyes.

Samita taught me that even the tiniest microbes work in and around our bodies to support life.

"Considerable damage is done on old Earth through harmful and toxic medication," she said. "Pharmaceuticals are used to destroy bacteria, fungi, and all the smallest organisms. In our ignorance, we failed to notice that microscopic helpers are necessary for rebuilding soil and maintaining health.

"Even our excrement is a vital part of the balance of nature. The bacteria-laden waste breaks down and is utilized as compost for the renewal of the land."

Sitting quietly together, Samita often appeared to converse with invisible entities.

"Fairies," she said, "work together with the plant kingdom. With the help of these invisible protectors, we can utilize nature for our needs without causing harm."

I thought about Veeda and the chicken broth, and Samita made a poignant observation.

"When we work for the good of all life, there is a synergy that occurs that can never be understood by the mind alone. There is a purpose to everything and a delicate balance amongst all life forms."

I believed I was beginning to understand.

Early one morning, sleeping in the meadow, I felt hot breath on my face. I opened my eyes and was nose to nose with the muzzle of a large grizzly bear. My heart thumped and my breath stopped. An overwhelming sensation of awe spiraled from the center of my chest down my legs and out my arms. The coarse fur tickled my cheeks and I stared into the warm brown eyes of the enormous beast.

He was curious and as we stared at each other, we shared a moment of gratitude. I wrapped my arms around his neck and the bear lowered himself toward me, careful not to crush me with his thousand-pound body. We embraced until the bear gently removed himself and lumbered into the forest. Samita was sitting quietly nearby.

"That was Grizzle," she said. "I was wondering when he was going to make an appearance. He's a wonder to behold, don't you think?"

I nodded, barely breathing, and we gazed at the sun, motionless. Samita breathed out a deep sigh of pain, apparently lost in a memory, and spoke out loud for the first time.

"We cannot destroy that which sustains us and expect to survive. It is against the laws of the universe and is the main reason old Earth will perish."

CHAPTER EIGHT

Malika

All things are possible, Rose.

Returning home, I felt a strong urge to see Malika.

Wearing a bright pink top and colorful skirt, Malika welcomed me warmly into her home. Her inviting dome offered a stark contrast to mine. While my tiny abode was open, light, and simple, Malika's screamed color and creativity. Mobiles of tinkling shells and crystals cast a sea of rainbows over the vibrant walls of bold and bright colors. The plush, curved sofa hugging the walls was filled with colorful pillows with fun textures. A tree touched the ceiling of her living room and hosted a small bird. The scent of cinnamon and cloves filled the room and I saw simmering spiced tea brewing in the kitchen.

Soft fur brushed my ankle, and I picked up a purring ginger cat who pushed her furry face into my hand.

"I'm a Creative," said Malika, "and that is Ginger." She stroked the cat in my arms.

It was apparent to me that Malika was a person of vast imagination. I had always admired people who could come up with fresh ideas seemingly out of thin air.

The cat jumped out of my arms.

"All things are possible, Rose," she said. "Creatives practice accessing the field of infinite possibility. Of course, this field is available to everyone; Creatives just have a deeper desire to connect with it. We inspire and build upon each other's ideas, let me show you."

Malika did a little hop and grabbed my hand, pulling me along outside her dome. Several large clay pots full of colorfully dyed leaves spread out in chaotic disarray. Rich turmeric yellow, beet red, and purple grape colors dripped from the vessels. Malika brought out baskets of shiny stones, shells, and delicately dried flowers. The irresistible array called to be arranged into beautiful works of art.

I couldn't resist getting my hands dirty and we spent the remainder of the day with our arms deep in colorful waters, staining our hands purplish-blue and creating marvelous designs. The infectious creative current swept us away and before I knew it, the evening gave way to night.

I visited Malika daily, always finding her immersed in new innovative projects that never failed to inspire me. Alaysia and Chestnut frequently joined us.

"Alaysia is a Creative like me," Malika said, "as well as a Nature Protector."

Together we spent many happy days creating brilliant works of art.

One day, I found Malika and Alaysia immersed in a sea of luxurious fabrics. Alaysia stood in front of Malika's hologram, her hair piled up on her head with purple strands cascading down in a tangled waterfall. She was designing a beautiful magenta gown covered in roses, altering the sleeves, and adjusting the length, lost in the enjoyment of the craft. Alaysia explained the textiles were woven from the delicate strands of spiderwebs sprinkled with the fine powder of gemstones.

After warm cups of chai tea with a splash of creamy hazelnut milk and a minor planning session, we spent the day producing costumes of exquisite loveliness.

Another day, I found Malika surrounded by piles of clay she had collected from the mountains in the outer reaches of Unity. The clays were green, blue, and deep, shiny black. During our pottery frenzy, we engraved each bowl, vase, and cup with intricate patterns and geometric designs. Alaysia sat cross-legged on the grass, carefully carving on her clay bowl.

"I've been going into the Central Hub to learn in the radiant domes," she said. "They're really fun. You might want to see them sometime."

She continued her artwork, and I stared at her, trying to understand why this young woman captivated me so.

One afternoon, alone with Malika, we nestled comfortably onto her couch. Cuddling Ginger and sipping fizzy purple starfruit soda, Malika shared about her visits to the art museums of San Francisco. She described a blue glowing tunnel made of a thousand glass triangles that she had seen at the Museum of Modern Art.

"It was incredible," she said. She paused to take a drink. "Old Earth didn't get everything wrong, just most things," she laughed. "One day, maybe, I'm going to help design new polycenters. I don't know," she shrugged. "It would be cool though, don't you think?"

Touched by her enthusiasm, I nodded in agreement. Putting my drink down, I asked, "I'm curious, how did you end up in Unity?"

"Well," she chuckled, "not nearly as dramatically as most Luminoles. I was living in a sweet little cottage in a small town in

California with my cats. I had a lovely art studio and a business helping others develop their creativity. I didn't listen to the news or care what was going on in the world. I got up every morning, read uplifting books, and focused on healing myself and creating the life of my dreams. My life just got better and better and everything flowed perfectly.

"One morning I woke up here, but honestly, it just seemed so natural. For a while, I didn't even notice that it was completely different. I started hearing other people's stories and I realized that I had been letting go of fear and judgment slowly and incrementally.

"My life here is hardly different; I'm still doing art and I'm still helping people access their creativity." She shrugged and looked at me. "We were great friends, you know."

Memories flooded back; years of long hikes, shared meals, and endless talking about nothing and everything. I fell into her arms, and we had a long, sweet hug.

Alaysia and Chestnut arrived, and we immersed ourselves in the latest project. I felt a happy flow with Malika and Alaysia creating together; it felt like old times.

After a satisfying day crafting beautiful artwork, Malika prepared all the things to be sent to the CDC. I watched her stack them carefully and neatly in her closet, sharing with Akashi the nature of the items. As she offered her gifts to the realm, Malika talked about how grateful she felt to be able to give back to the community.

"Unity has given me so much," she said, "I sometimes wish I could give more." She clapped her hands together triumphantly as the wares flew off to the Central Hub.

Alysia and I had just started walking home when Oriane arrived. She was with a bearded middle-aged man in a striking burgundy robe with platinum trim. He wore a yarmulka on his bald head and was trailed by a large black wolf. Oriane introduced Peretz as her bond-mate and explained that they all had ascended as a family some time ago.

"Peretz is a Creative Builder and works in the Central Hub designing structures and innovative technology," said Oriane.

I caught a sparkle in his eye and had a subtle flash of recognition, quickly discarded. With self-assured humility, Peretz gave me a nod of respect before departing with Alaysia.

Oriane walked me home, knowing I held a question in my heart.

"Everyone here gives me so much," I said, "and I'm not giving anything back. I feel kind of, well, lazy and selfish. I wonder if I should be doing something, but I'm not sure what that might be."

Oriane looked at me with a stern and serious face.

"Rose, it is imperative that you take all the time you need to heal and explore," she said firmly. "Giving out of guilt will taint your gifts. In the old world, we almost always give with a need to get something back. There is always a need for reciprocity—like money, acknowledgment, power, or fame.

"In Unity, 'working' is a gift and is done out of a pure desire to share. Your soul must be full for your gifts to flourish. At some point, you will feel a deep desire to give. Then, and only then, will you be ready. Until that time, you *must* follow your impulses as they arise."

Relieved, I nodded my understanding.

Oriane grinned playfully and said, "I believe it is time for your welcome party!"

CHAPTER NINE

Welcome Party

It is essential that you recognize your magnificence.

I flushed, feeling hot at the thought of being welcomed by a bunch of, mostly, strangers. Oriane said that embarrassment is just a remnant of old Earth unworthiness, and I went to bed dreaming up my outfit and a tasty morsel to share with my new friends.

The day of the party, I had a lovely morning with Malika, designing a simple silver flowing gown in the Akashi hologram. She giggled, rolling her eyes when I refused to allow her to add extra sparkle.

Aspen shared a recipe for purple starfruit pie and Alaysia came over to help me bake. We playfully painted purple juice on our noses, laughing as Chestnut pulled on the cuff of her bedazzled jeans, wishing for a bite of the juicy fruit.

Electric energy pulsed in the heart of Azure Village. It was clear that everyone loved a party and all the Luminoles bustled about in cheerful preparation. Dara, Jax, and Greta hung fairy lights in the trees. Villagers sprawled on the grass, busily crafting colorful rice paper decorations. Aspen, along with other Culinary Creatives, spent hours in their kitchens preparing a sumptuous feast.

I took an afternoon nap before making my way to the party. Joyous melodies, from musically inclined Creatives, reverberated from the village center. The garden was especially vibrant as colorful, softly glowing rice paper lanterns hovered above the greenery. The usual floral scent was overpowered by the enticing aromas coming from bubbling pots and freshly baked towers of sweets.

Malika arrived in a lavish gown with fine pink stripes and was the first to offer a warm hug. Alaysia, in a stunning dress of roses, was playing with Chestnut, Dara, and Akira until they saw me and ran over to smother me with hugs. All the Luminoles of the village, clad in ivory or whatever colorful outfit suited their fancy, drifted into the jubilee, filled with anticipation.

Magna kicked off the festivities with a grand performance. In her full expression, she enacted a story from old Earth about the insanity of 'work.' She pretended to wallow in drudgery, working a job that didn't align with her soul. Magna shape-shifted with ease to play multiple characters at one time. Everyone roared with laughter at her outrageous antics, recalling memories of old Earth.

Her production was like a live three-dimensional movie, and I realized how limited my old reality had been.

Greta and Alfred sat behind me sniggering, and I felt a gentle hand on my back. I turned as Alfred spoke to me. "I'm sure you can relate," he said, nodding his head.

Greta patted his knee and took a deep breath. "As can we, my love, as can we," she said. They looked at each other with knowing eyes before joining the festivities.

The healing laughter lifted my spirit, and I was effortlessly able to enjoy the rest of the party.

Culinary Creatives brought out savory stews, marinated mushrooms, and thinly sliced herbed vegetables to tickle our palates. Cake towers made with roasted cacao and sweetened with the natural sugars of purple starfruit were arranged in elaborate designs. Petunia and Chestnut joined in the merriment. Everyone danced with wild abandon to the music that filled the garden. Merry-berry wine was passed around, and cuddles were doled out liberally amongst the exuberant fervor.

As dusk fell, Jax turned into a magnificent dragon, brilliant red with shining iridescent scales and majestic wings. The dragon blew plumes of harmless fire into the sky over and over that turned into showers of sparkling raindrops. Our cheeks and clothes shimmered briefly before melting away. The dragon turned back into Jax, and the music faded as we all melted into a sea of contentment.

* * *

I sat alone on the grass as the guests departed for home. Overwhelmed by the reception, the spirited hugs, and the frivolity all in my honor; I felt like a celebrity but did not feel deserving of such hoopla. Oriane was at my side instantly, reminding me of the old Earth unworthiness trap.

Oriane gently took my hands and looked at me with intensity. "It is essential that you recognize your magnificence," she said. "As you can see, we all know it and soon you will find it within. You can only offer your gifts to this world when you fully accept your divinity and worth."

Sensing the deep respect she had for my process, I shuffled around in discomfort.

"No one is above or below another," she said. "We are all unique and while we may have differing levels of skill and knowledge, Unity is a realm of oneness and profound equality."

Looking deeply into my eyes, she placed her fingertips on my heart and encouraged me to go to The Crescent Healing Center the next day.

CHAPTER TEN

Maanya

You are now free to claim your rightful place as equal to all other beings.

The next morning, I donned my simple ivory tunic, snuggled into my chair with a hot, sweet, chicory beverage full of creamy almond milk, and pondered the previous night. The inundation of adoration had triggered buried feelings from old Earth that wished to be dislodged.

I trudged to The Crescent amidst a gentle rain. When I arrived at the gardens, I knelt for a moment at the pond, splashing my face with the sparkling sweet water. I had a drink and, refreshed, inspected the building.

It dawned on me at that moment, why it was called The Crescent. The structure encircled three-quarters of the garden and was fatter in the middle, where the entryway stood, and receded into gentle sloping points on each end like a large croissant. Appreciating the creativity of the Luminoles and the beauty of the garden, I knew I could procrastinate no further.

One of the blue Healers I had met on my first day was waiting for me in the atrium. At our first meeting, for some reason, it didn't occur to me that she did *not* look human. She was tall and thin and had an ethereal blue glow. The bodysuit she wore blended in with her skin. She had large sparkling eyes filled with wisdom.

"I am Maanya," she said. "I am from the eleventh dimension of the Pleiadian Star System and, along with my companions, came here to help build this world called Unity. For many years we have been assisting Earth with this transition. My role here in Unity is a Healer. I assist Luminoles when they arrive and train the Healers of Elysia. I offer my gifts to help you grow and evolve following your soul's desire."

I had no words. Engulfed in an overwhelming sense of safety and love, I felt held in a mother's embrace. She guided me to the same healing room I went to when I initially arrived. We sat together and she shared.

"You have been experiencing unworthiness. It is an energy from old Earth that is perpetuated to establish dominance by those-that-seek-to-control. They themselves carry so much fear that they believe their only option is to oppress others to elevate themselves. You have been subjected to thousands of years of programming and have been told that you are less.

"Through movies, advertising, and even religion, you have been instilled with subtle messages telling you that you are bad, undeserving, and unlovable. This creates a necessary drama on old Earth that is vital for learning and growing, however, now, here in Unity, it is no longer necessary. You are now free to claim your rightful place as equal to all other beings. Discovering this truth, you can begin to find your unique gifts that are so needed in this world.

"Come, I will help you release this old programming that is still lodged in your cellular structure."

She led me to the Cocoon, and I crawled in, curling up like a small child. Realizing the gravity of her words, a profound sadness came over me. Maanya placed her hands gently on my back and started to vibrate and hum. As the magnitude of the deception finally sank in, I sobbed out mountains of pain, eons of suffering, and lifetimes of believing a lie.

CHAPTER ELEVEN

Drake, Viola, Yeshua, and Hannah

In ancient times on old Earth, the priests and priestesses served as sexual healers.

Weary after my healing with Maanya, I wandered through the village, savoring the gentle glow of the evening. The earthy scent of pine, sweetened with rose seemed especially pronounced. Miriam and Lina's gentle lullaby permeated the night and a peaceful calm descended. As I passed a large home that reminded me of a temple, I saw four bodies weaving in and throughout the lush garden.

I watched four Luminoles sway gracefully and then begin to dance, their movements intertwined in sensuous fluidity. Still woozy from my session with Maanya, I stood perfectly still. Closing my eyes I sensed the rhythmic vibrations of their erotic display. When I opened my eyes, I found myself surrounded.

A tall man with deep, brown eyes and soft, silky, black hair introduced himself as Drake.

"We haven't had the pleasure of welcoming you to Azure Village," he said. "These are my bond-mates, Viola, Yeshua, and Hannah. We are pleased you're here."

I glanced at the four Luminoles and Drake responded to my thoughts. "We share our sexuality and also offer ourselves to the community," he said.

A whisper of judgment flitted into my consciousness as I thought of prostitutes and brothels of old Earth.

"That's a common response," Drake said. "But, like everything, there are higher and lower vibrations of sexuality. In ancient times on old Earth, the priests and priestesses served as sexual healers.

"The youth entering sexual maturity went to them to receive training. Young men were taught to manage sexual desire and hold their seed. Acquiring techniques to please their partner and enhance their own, they came to understand the healing power of sexuality. Young women attuned to the signals of their bodies and learned to regulate reproduction.

"It was a great service and allowed those civilizations to function without the sexual perversions that are so pervasive on old Earth."

As my judgments melted away, I wished to know more.

Hannah, the smallest of the four, had a small, supple body, long black hair, and eyes of deep brown sparkling pools of wisdom. Fragile and shy, she spoke softly, sharing her story.

"I spent my childhood in Guatemala," she said. "Like many families fleeing violence, we attempted to cross the border illegally when I was only eight years old. Separated from my parents at the border, I was kidnapped and sold into a life of sex trafficking. I was offered as a commodity to high-powered senators, movie stars, and foreign dignitaries. I became pregnant at age eleven and was forced to give up my child. I lived half a life, and, in my misery, I reached out to the only thing I knew.

"Having been raised Catholic, I prayed, begging for release and an end to my nightmare. After years of abuse, my prayers were granted. Mary Magdalene, in all her beauty and wisdom, appeared to me. She merged with me, and from that moment, Mary Magdalene became my closest ally. She taught me about the great power of sexuality, showing me that those who came for sexual gratification were merely broken children in need of healing. My communion with Mary Magdalene healed me and over the years, I released lifetimes of sexual trauma.

"Through the grace of Mary Magdalene, my body became impervious to disease and accidental pregnancy. I no longer experienced my sexual duties as a painful burden. I began to utilize my newfound wisdom to plant a seed in the hearts of those who sought to use my body for their gratification. My greatest pain became my greatest offering, and I was a highly sought-after sexual healer, much like the priests and priestesses of the ancient civilizations."

Hannah paused, looking at me with soft eyes.

"After ascending to Unity," she said. "I was drawn together with Drake, Viola, and Yeshua. Their stories are nearly identical to mine and we bonded instantly."

Examining the four, I sensed no trace of sexual wounding, only strength, wisdom, purity, and depth.

* * *

Cozy in my bed, I gazed at the stars, awash with the fragile emptiness of receptivity. Hand on my belly, the space that had once been filled with pain was now a well-spring of creativity and healing. Hannah's transmission had miraculously filled my empty cup. Falling into dreamless slumber, I was nowhere to be found.

CHAPTER TWELVE

Veeda

When the desire to have a child happens, we call in the perfect soul who is a vibrational match.

One warm afternoon after a satisfying swim in the lake, I snuggled into the comfy softness of my living room chair, wrapped in a blanket. Hearing the rustling of activity outside, I paused for a moment and contemplated remaining in my cozy chair. But the cheerful levity echoing from the heart of Azure Village was irresistible and I set out to investigate.

Dara and Akira danced about with three boys, all with masses of curly locks. A colorful musical Creative, clothed in elaborate embroidery, played an unusual stringed instrument and sang songs about purple elephants and rainbow-colored lizards. Alaysia jumped up and down, her burgundy smock fluttering in the breeze, and laughed as Chestnut tried to follow suit. Jax was doing graceful flips, unencumbered by xyr enormous weight.

Leaning up against a tree, enjoying the whimsical scene, I watched the children play.

Veeda, a soft, warm presence who I knew to be Aspen's bond-mate, had a cream-colored ferret curled around her graceful neck and wrapped her arm in mine. Leaning into me, she gazed at her children.

"All three of my boys were born here in Unity," she said. Looking upon the curly lot with deep affection, she told me that Cedar was her eldest at age twelve; then Summit, ten; and Puma, five.

"Immediately after I ascended, I bonded with Aspen," she said. "We both had a great desire to parent as did our friends, Baz, and Josiah." She indicated two men who were dancing with the children. "Together, we called in the souls of our children."

I looked at her, my brow furrowed.

"When the desire to have a child happens," she said, "we call in the perfect soul who is a vibrational match. Most couples in Unity only have one or two children to give them the full attention they deserve. But our desire together, compelled us to have four."

I glanced up at the three energetic boys and looked back at her.

"Four?" I asked.

"I am pregnant with our daughter, Viviana," she said and looked down, flushing. She brushed her long dark hair behind her ear and smoothed down her ivory tunic, softly touching her flat belly.

I smiled at her, sensing her pleasure, and she caressed the cocoon of her tiny embryo.

"Waaa! Again, again!" Puma screamed as Baz threw him up in the air and then swung him around, landing a few feet from us.

"Hi, I'm Sebastian. Call me Baz," said the tall, muscular man as Puma screamed for more. Baz held out his hand and I shook it. "I'm with him," he pointed to Josiah who looked over at us and waved, "sexually, I mean." He brushed his sweaty brown waves from his face. "But we are with Veeda here and Aspen, parentally speaking. They gifted us with our three awesome boys." He grabbed Puma, who was unrelenting in his insistence, and threw him into the air again.

Josiah, a man, small in stature with short, black, tight curls came over and offered a warm hug. He rejoined his bond-mate and the kids, now a large group, and proceeded to toss a little one onto his shoulders, inciting squeals of delight.

"Between the four of us," said Veeda, "we offer them more than any one of us alone. Josiah and Baz are both Educators, Jax mentors them."

Veeda looked over at Josiah and then went to whisper something to him. Josiah turned to me as though struck with a brilliant idea.

"I'd love to show you what we do," he said. "It's nothing like old Earth. The kids love coming to school and we can make a real difference in their lives."

CHAPTER THIRTEEN

Education

It is simply understood that they are valued, and their contribution matters.

Unity offers education to all Luminoles and their children." That evening, cozied in my chair, sipping herbal tea, I asked Akashi about the education system of Unity. "I can assist you in finding all available educational opportunities," she said.

An extensive list appeared in the middle of my living room: nature studies, culinary delights, spelunking, creative building, crystal technology, reproduction and bonding. The abundance of opportunities fascinated me. Categorized by age and location, I found the class I wanted and made my plans for the next day.

The next morning, I woke early and headed over to Serene Lake where the Educators were preparing a lesson on herbal healing for a group of tweens. The squirrelly children arrived, chatting enthusiastically.

Dara came up to me and gave me a spontaneous hug. "What are you doing here?" she asked. She looked pleased to see me.

"Well, I'm curious how school happens here," I said. "It's different from old Earth."

"Don't let Puma hear you mention old Earth," she said, "or he will never let you stop talking. He's obsessed you know, with old Earth I mean."

I looked around.

"Don't worry, he's not here today," she said.

Akira came over and Dara skipped away.

"What do you like about school here?" I asked Akira after she gave me a hug. Her gentle energy was soothing to me, and I thought she might give me some answers.

"Oh, school is fun. Today, we are going on an herb walk. I love herbs." She took a caterpillar from her hair and placed it gently on a tree, telling it to be careful.

"Jax usually turns into some kind of animal," she said. "I hope it's a unicorn today, that's my favorite." She smiled softly then turned back to the tree and encouraged the caterpillar onto her hand.

The kids were rounded up and we began an exploration among the trees, collecting berries, leaves, and bark. As we gathered medicinals, some familiar to me, Josiah shared their energetic properties.

Stopping in a clearing, Baz pulled out materials to make salves and tinctures. I settled myself onto a curved rock and observed as the children immersed themselves in the craft. Akira and Leaf, a non-binary from the Central Hub, had made a comfrey salve and Baz was showing them a gentle massage technique. Leaf giggled and massaged Akira's hand as Akira offered advice on pressure and depth.

Summit and other children ran about collecting buckets of elderberries for syrup. A young boy with a large fuzzy afro was perched on a fallen tree trunk and conversed with a small gray squirrel, who was standing in the folds of his ivory tunic.

Cedar had climbed high up a tree to gather pine needles for tea and Dara stood on the branch next to him, handing him bushy twigs. Just as he swung from his knees, the pockets of his deep green overalls spilling over, Josiah appeared to offer assistance and Cedar flipped down from the tree in a graceful dismount. Josiah held out his arms and Dara jumped into them before running off with Cedar.

Hands on his hips, Josiah sighed and smiled. He looked at me and walked over. "What do you think?" he asked.

"I love to see the kids so engaged," I said.

"Yup, I taught in the inner city of New York, and this is a dream come true," he said. "I used to pour useless information into the kids' heads and expected them to regurgitate it. I knew there was a better way, I just didn't know how to make a change. The kids were always so bored. No wonder, we didn't have a clue how to inspire them."

He sighed and I detected a painful story.

After a few hours, Jax, ready to end the lesson, gathered the children.

WOOSH!!

I turned around to behold a magnificent, iridescent pink unicorn with a shiny horn that sparkled in the light. Jax cantered around gathering energy and helped them focus. Their delighted faces began to calm, and Jax, the unicorn, gently and skillfully guided the children into centered calmness.

I joined in and felt my thoughts coalesce. As we all settled down, Jax slowly returned to xyr original form.

Making our way back to Serene Lake, Akira exclaimed, "Just think of all the ways we are going to be able to help the new Luminoles!" Scooping up a small fox that begged to be held, she nuzzled his fur.

"Why are they called Luminoles?" I asked.

Cedar stopped walking and piped in with the answer. "Puma, my little brother, and I were at the Healing Center," he said. "We saw some newcomers arrive and they were glowing." He brushed the wild curls from his face, and I sat down to fully receive his words.

"I told Puma that they looked 'luminous,' and he started calling them Luminoles," he said. "Now that's what everyone calls them. And you are too now, a Luminole I mean." He shrugged.

Reaching into his pocket, Cedar handed me a small wooden butterfly.

"I made this for you," he said, with a half-smile. He turned, did a backflip, then jogged off to join his friends.

After inspecting the intricate details, I held the stunning treasure to my heart, reflecting on the word, 'Luminoles.' I felt a rosy warm glow and my sense of belonging solidified.

Back at Serene Lake, the waters were alive with activity. Luminoles splashed and swam, paddled in boats and practiced windsurfing.

We retreated to a quiet location and Jax initiated a playful lesson. He was going to show them how to alter their hair using nothing but the power of their thoughts. As the children sat in quiet contemplation, I observed with curiosity.

Following Jax's soothing and skillful instructions, the children were drawn into focused attention. At first, nothing seemed to be happening. Cedar, Akira, and Dara sat with calm serenity but some of the other children scrunched up their faces in effort.

Akira was the first to succeed. Her braids began to get longer, slowly at first, and eventually, she managed to grow them to the ground. Dara soon followed suit and after that, all the children were able to change their hair length at will.

When Leaf succeeded in changing to a fiery orange, suddenly a burst of color started popping out of all heads; blue, neon green, long, and then short. When Cedar suddenly created a fuzzy pink mass of curly locks, he put everyone into fits of giggles. A wild burst of creativity ensued, and the hairstyles got increasingly outrageous.

When one child went bald then suddenly blue and purple pigtails erupted poking straight out of their bald head, no one could hold back and we were all laughing so hard, tears were rolling down our cheeks. I fell off the rock and belly laughed. It took many moments to catch my breath.

After the lively lesson, the children squealed and ran into the lake, some shedding their tunics with abandon, unaffected by shame or self-consciousness. As I watched the children scream and splash into the late afternoon, Josiah sat next to me on the sand. We sat silently for some time as the golden light sparkled on the pristine waters. He seemed immensely pleased and satisfied, and I wondered how all this happened with such ease.

"Is there some kind of curriculum?" I asked.

"Nope, nothing like that," he said. "Just like everything here in Unity, it is all very organic. It took a while for me to trust the process. I kept having the urge to create some kind of lesson plan to establish order. But when you trust the flow, everyone's needs get met. I know that sounds like woo woo jargon, but it is really true here.

"So, each night before class, sometimes I know a few days in advance, I think about what I most want to teach and post on Akashi's education board. We provide classes for all the children of Elysia. Baz and Jax do the same. It just so happens that we've been aligned lately and the three of us teach together most days.

"Jax is a master. I've never experienced the level of compassion that Jax has for these kids. I'm often moved to tears, to be honest. Baz and I are always talking about xem. I can't even imagine the good that could be done on old Earth if we had teachers like Jax."

"How do the kids choose classes?" I asked.

"The children and their parents decide together based on the child's needs. It changes daily. The classes are always full, and it is always exactly the right mix of kids who most need to be there. When kids reach adolescence, they choose for themselves, like my son Cedar there."

I looked over at the boy doing handstands on the sand, his curly locks flailing about.

"He is already designing his own educational pathway," he said, looking at his son with an air of wonder. "All they know is love and respect. It is simply understood that they are valued, and their contribution matters."

* * *

In the days that followed, I never once saw a bored child. It was always a different mix of kids, and I loved seeing the variation. Sometimes it was Josiah or Baz alone, teaching a couple of kids, but usually, the three taught together. Observing the educators, I understood more fully Josiah's deep admiration for Jax.

While Josiah and Baz had old Earth experience as teachers and brought a wealth of knowledge, Jax held the essential foundation of love, acceptance, and compassion. When classes became chaotic, Jax became just the right animal to teach the kids a powerful lesson. Baz was a Creative and always came up with engaging and unique art projects. Josiah's gentle presence effortlessly soothed a frustrated child with a simple touch on the back. Together, the three created a perfect balance and I understood why they chose to work together.

One day, an unfamiliar Educator named Shakk, dressed in orange overalls, visited us from the Central Hub to offer a class in telekinesis.

"Moving things with your mind is especially helpful for us Builders," she said, "because we can move heavy objects without needing machinery."

She demonstrated her skill to the wide-eyed children. With keen attention, I observed a large rock jiggle and wiggle and then eventually, float, landing gently on an even larger boulder. One by one, rocks floated up, creating a small, geometrically aligned structure. Gasping, all the kids settled onto the grass, eager to learn this new skill.

Shakk was new to teaching and after some clunky guidance, only Cedar succeeded in bouncing a small pebble up and down. This distracted the children for a moment until everyone realized that Ismar was levitating.

Ismar had scooped up a squirrel in a tall tree and gently floated back down. Without realizing what he had done, the sensitive boy settled himself back on the grass, snuggling the furry animal that was desperately trying to burrow into his impressive afro. All the children gathered around bewildered Ismar, asking him how he had managed the feat. He glanced up in surprise at the crowd around him and laughed.

"I didn't even know I could do that!" he breathed. "It just... happened! I saw Frizzle in the tree trying to reach me and I just wanted to help him so I just. . . just, floated up and got him!"

It was obvious he had astonished himself and all the children chatted happily, forgetting the task at hand.

* * *

These children had all been born into Unity and had no vestiges of pain. They were unaffected by doubt or shame. Reflecting on old Earth, sadness welled up, sparking a fervent wish for all children to have this opportunity. As I watched the youth, full of laughter and creativity, a flame of hope for humanity that had almost all but disappeared, ignited once again.

CHAPTER FOURTEEN

The Central Hub of Elysia

You see, there is no objective reality, only that which we create with our thoughts.

After a fun class making adhesives with snail mucin and sap, I chatted with Leaf, a ten-year-old with a pixie haircut and a playful smile. Leaf's enthusiastic description of the Central Hub of Elysia piqued my curiosity. That evening, while sitting in my warm bath, Akashi generated vibrant images of a stunning polycenter.

"The inhabitants of Unity are called Luminoles," said Akashi. "You live in the outland village of Azure in the polycenter of Elysia, one of many outland villages that surround the Central Hub. There are currently fifty-three polycenters in Unity."

Upon Oriane's suggestion, we planned a visit to the Central Hub of Elysia. The following morning, Oriane and I walked through The Crescent and out the back archway. We came upon a flat, circular platform about twenty feet in diameter. Miriam and Lina were already there waiting.

"This is our transportation system," said Oriane. "It's called The Whisper."

"You are visiting the Central Hub for the first time?" asked Miriam, more of a statement than a question.

I nodded, smiling at her. An eager buzz danced about in my belly.

"Well, you are in for a treat," she said.

We stepped onto the platform and waited for a moment. I glanced around, wondering what might happen. Oriane looked up with a huge grin. My eyes followed her gaze as a small, silent, spheroid object appeared above our heads.

The sleek vessel hovered several feet above us and a ramp gracefully unfolded and hooked into a small opening on the platform. We all climbed onto the hovercraft and settled into our comfortable seats. Sitting in a circle we all faced each other.

"The four-seater Whisper is the smallest available for journeys around Elysia," said Oriane, "but there are larger vessels too. Some travel to other polycenters. The entire transport system is controlled by Akashi and no driver is needed."

I looked around at the simplicity of the vessel and, out of habit, searched for my seatbelt. Oriane laughed.

"Nope, no seatbelt required," she said.

The seat lounged back into a comfortable bed and a small tray was available within the armrest. I reclined the seat fully and gazed up at the smooth, round ceiling. Putting my seat back up, I took the tray out and set my arms upon it. Oriane watched me with an amused grin. Lina and Miriam chuckled.

"No windows?" I asked.

"The smallest vessel has no windows," said Oriane, "but the larger ones have a viewing portal."

I remembered how much I enjoyed flying on old Earth. Eventually, oil had become too expensive and commercial flights were stopped. But before that, flying had always filled me with the promise of something new and exciting. I put the tray back in its 'up-right position' before departure and smiled to myself.

"We're here," said Oriane.

"Really, already?" I looked around, realizing I had been anticipating a rush of inertia.

The side of the vessel opened, and we waited for Miriam and Lina before exiting onto a much larger round platform.

Still enamored with my hovercraft, I inspected the details of the ramp. I appreciated the perfection of the workmanship and watched my feet as I walked. I marveled at the smoothness of the landing plate and recognized the technological brilliance of the hook to which the ramp was now attached.

Oriane gently touched my hand, and I looked up. I took a step back and my breath stopped. My brain simply could not process what I was seeing.

My mouth fell wide open, and I gasped audibly. Though I was looking at a city, I felt like I had stepped into a futuristic novel and was now a cartoon character in a fantasy world. I was glad that I had peed before the journey, because perhaps I would have lost it if my bladder was full. Oriane appeared to be enjoying my amazement.

"It never fails to stop my breath," she said. "It is incredible, isn't it?"

I nodded, dumbfounded. Though it was definitely a city, much of the natural wildness remained. Strategically placed buildings left bushes, splashed with color, and giant trees intact. I craned my neck to gape at the spiraling towers, draped with fresh greenery and another Whisper hovercraft whizzed by.

Majestic waterfalls cascading from the structures sprayed my face with sweet water. The intricate latticework of the graceful arches painted dapples of sunlight over the warm marble walkways.

Remembering to breathe, I filled my lungs with crisp air. The enticing aromas of Culinary Creatives' cuisine complemented the thick fragrance of jasmine.

"Just look at what we can accomplish when we work together for the good of all," Oriane said with a deep sigh of contentment.

Humming with activity, the Central Hub was alive with vibrant energy. Children played in fountains, splashing, and singing. Adults immersed in art, games, or deep conversation convened in grassy knolls and on bridges over the crystalline river. Passing Luminoles welcomed us with warm smiles and nods. Strolling the Central Hub, Oriane shared facts about Unity

"Each polycenter in the realm of Unity is unique," she said. "They reflect the wishes and desires of the Luminoles that live there. Elysia was one of the first polycenters. It is one of the few that has reached full capacity. New Luminoles come in only when other residents leave, so we now maintain a constant population."

As we relaxed in a grassy area near a small bubbling fountain, we savored some delicacies that had been generously offered; luscious deep red fruit pastries and soft cheeses made of fermented nuts. Feeling satisfied and well nourished, I laid on the grass.

Staring up at the pale blue sky, I asked Oriane, "You call Unity a 'realm,' but, isn't Unity a planet just like Earth?"

Oriane finished her pastry. "I call it a realm," she said, "because it is in the process of being created by the intentions of the Luminoles. You see, there is no objective reality. There is only that which we create with our thoughts. Thoughts are the creative force of the universe, so changes in thought correspond to shifts in reality."

I pondered this for a moment. This was not a new concept for me, but to hear it from her, today, now, in *this* reality, it impacted me differently. Did I create Unity with my thoughts? What happens when my thoughts miraculously stop? Clearly beyond the understanding of the mind alone, truths went deeper than I ever imagined.

Recharged from our brunch, Oriane suggested we visit Harmony Healing Center. I was up for anything and we fed our leftovers to the birds before wiping the grass from our bottoms. Oriane suddenly glanced at me with a heavy look on her face. Reaching for my arm, we took a couple steps before she revealed a terrible truth.

"The wars are ramping up on Earth," she said. She looked incredibly sad. "This means we will be expecting large numbers of new Luminoles. They will all be directly transported to the Healing Centers before finding their appropriate homes."

Oriane's step lightened. "Come, I'll show you Harmony," she said. "It's magnificent, and you can meet Ronan and Azriel, my dear friends."

CHAPTER FIFTEEN

Harmony Healing Center

Just as a butterfly must let go of its caterpillar-ness, similarly we must release everything we imagined ourselves to be to transform into Luminoles.

Harmony reminded me of The Crescent in its sublime tranquility, only much larger. We walked among the greenery and flowers of the atrium, bathed in subtle alpha waves while waiting for Oriane's friends.

Sitting on the edge of a fountain, I saw a tall man with long blonde hair in ivory robes gliding towards us. He warmly embraced Oriane.

"Oriane, it is such a pleasure to see you again," he said and then turned to welcome me with his eyes, nodding a greeting.

"This is my dear friend Ronan," said Oriane. Turning to him she asked, "Will Azriel be joining us today?"

Just then, a towering man, also in classic ivory, strode into the plaza, tying up his silky dreadlocks. Azriel had a deep purple crystal hanging around his neck. His eyes were cool, but his countenance was kind. He simply nodded with calm confidence. Taken aback by the stunning musculature of the two men, I quickly relaxed when I perceived their warmth and humility. Ronan led us into a spacious greenhouse, teeming with vibrant flora, the air saturated with the earthy scent of medicinal herbs.

"Every plant in this greenhouse holds unique healing properties," said Ronan. "Nature Protectors help us." He gestured to the Luminoles sitting quietly amongst the foliage. "They communicate with the plant spirits to learn of their uses and then share that knowledge."

"Plant spirits?" I asked.

"Some call them fairies, 'plant spirits' is just my term," he said. "All life forms have invisible protectors, and if we are sensitive enough, we can connect with them."

I thought of Samita and everything she had taught me. I was delightfully amused to hear a golden god-like man that reminded me of Thor, talk about fairies.

Ronan touched a thick stem and followed it with his eyes to the towering glass ceiling. Tracking his gaze, I saw an unusual plant; a wild feathery mass covered with small round nuts.

"This is the kakua plant," he said. "It produces a nut that makes a great lubricant." He found a small container on a crowded shelf and poured a drop of slippery liquid onto each of our hands. "It's wonderful for sexual play." Oriane and I smiled and nodded as we rubbed the silky substance between our fingers.

Azriel stood by quietly as Ronan guided us around the greenhouse, naming plants and telling us of their medicinal properties. I tuned him out after a while and simply appreciated the beauty. After the greenhouse tour, we stood at the entrance.

"I was an arrogant doctor on old Earth and almost descended to hell because of it," said Ronan. "My wife was the one who shook me awake. She loves plants and had filled our home with them. I had thought it was cute at the time, not realizing the healing potential. Now, I am only just beginning to appreciate everything she tried to teach me.

"She ascended first, of course, but fortune smiled upon me, and we bonded, once I extracted my head from my anal sphincter." Oriane and I laughed and Azriel rolled his eyes.

"My bond-mate is also a Healer," said Ronan. "She is in the middle of a healing session, or I'd introduce you."

"You've already met her," said Oriane. "Nora is his bond-mate, Miriam and Lina's younger sister." I recalled the singing, floating sisters and nodded.

Azriel took over the tour. Standing outside a new door he shared his passion with us.

"Ronan and I went to medical school together," he said. "After we ascended, he gravitated towards plants, but I fell in love with the mineral kingdom."

He opened the door to a large room filled with dazzling crystals; soft translucent rose quartz, deep purple amethyst, and ivory moonstone. The soft, warm glow of the room enhanced the colors, casting iridescent halos around the circular space. Azriel picked up a stone from a table and showed it to us.

"This is black tourmaline, it's my favorite stone here," he said.

Azriel offered the stone, and I held out my hand. It was a soft black oval and felt nice in my palm. I handed it back to Azriel.

"Black tourmaline protects your energy field and promotes relaxation," he said, putting the stone back into its velvety nest. "All the stones here have a healing influence, just like Ronan's plants."

I walked around the room picking up crystals and putting them down. I had always loved gem shows on old Earth and felt like a kid in a candy store.

"I've spent many years trying to understand the healing potential of these precious minerals," said Azriel. "I used to be a trauma surgeon and, like Ronan, had been completely unaware of the power of nature to heal."

He picked up a sparkling amethyst skull and turned it around looking at it with a similar reverence to Ronan and his plants.

"I now understand that the power of the crystal is reflected by its beauty, these phenomenal crystalline gems emerged from the body of our mother; can you imagine?"

We walked silently through Harmony's warmly glowing halls and came upon a healing in progress. Quietly observing, I saw three Healers encircling a new Luminole.

I peered in and palpable vibrations raised the hairs on my arms. A beautiful young woman was curled in a Cocoon, her long blonde tresses cascading over the pillow. Nora, Ronan's bond-mate, and her sisters, floated in a rotating circle above the Cocoon, serenading the newest Luminole with their haunting melody.

Ronan softly whispered, "This newcomer was a very famous singer on old Earth," he said.

Scrutinizing the woman, she appeared noticeably young, and I sensed a wisdom beyond her years. We left the room, quietly closing the door.

"Those-that-seek-to-control tried to use her fame to elevate themselves," he said. "She had a really traumatic life and died of illness in a sanctuary city."

"She looks so young, how old is she?" I asked.

"She's twelve years old," he said.

I glanced back at the closed door in shock. "I thought children never ascend. I thought they could only be born," I said.

"That's usually the case, but this one grew up so fast, her soul somehow made it right before she died," said Ronan.

Before our tour was complete, Azriel and Ronan led us to a large room with twelve Cocoons arranged in a perfect circle.

"Collective healings take place here," said Ronan.

"Healings like this are required to unravel group trauma, such as in times of war," said Azriel.

Oriane turned to me. "Only a very powerful Healer can facilitate such an event," she said, her eyes sparkling. "It requires great skill to bring about that kind of transformation."

"I doubt I will ever participate in that kind of healing," said Ronan, "I prefer plant medicine. Once a Luminole is awake and aware, I bring them herbs to help heal the physical."

"Same for me," said Azriel. "After the Cocoon healings, the physical body is much more receptive to herbs and crystals, and we can heal all manner of issues."

I inspected the Cocoons, noticing for the first time that they appeared to hover. Running my hands over the smooth surface I peered under the egg. There was just enough space between the bed and a small round landing plate on the floor for my hand to fit.

Caressing the soft underbelly, I was reminded of The Whisper and asked how it worked.

"It's technology from the extraterrestrials," said Azriel, "the same as that of the hovercraft. The landing plate is a mini-crystal grid, it connects to the network within the Cocoon to make it hover. But it goes even further; when a Luminole enters the Cocoon, Akashi scans the physical body for illness and injury."

Azriel pulled up an Akashi hologram and I saw an image of a body spinning slowly. He toggled through different Luminoles and showed us how various areas of damage lit up with red.

"Initially, Akashi would just verbally diagnose," he said, "but now, we can connect mentally and get a physical readout of everything happening in the cellular structures. Minerals in the bed are geometrically aligned for optimal healing."

"Is there a special reason they're called Cocoons?" I asked. "Does it have a cover of some kind?"

"No, they remain open. It just seems like a perfect metaphor," said Ronan. "You know, when the caterpillar enters a cocoon, well, he doesn't just sprout wings. He must completely melt down and transform everything about himself to become. . ."

"A butterfly," Oriane and I said at the same time.

"Exactly," smiled Ronan. "Just as a butterfly must let go of its caterpillar-ness, similarly we must release everything we imagined ourselves to be to transform into Luminoles."

We finished our tour and retreated to a small grassy courtyard to share a meal. We passed around various fruits, nuts, and delicious berry bark buns. Ronan brought out an herbal elixir that he claimed would ensure a restful night. Passing around the concoction, the Healers reflected on the medical system of old Earth.

"I've seen the power of crystals to stop bleeding, close wounds, and even shrink tumors," said Azriel. "My old Earth surgical techniques seem so barbaric in comparison; if it wasn't so sad, it would be comical." A tremble crossed his lips as he squinted into the sun.

"In Unity," said Ronan, "we empower individuals to care for the body." He took a sip of his herbal drink and turned towards me. "Even kids are taught anatomy early on and understand this principle."

The Healers kept bringing the conversation back to their chosen modality, as if in competition to determine whose method was best. Thoroughly enjoying the lively discussion, I was pleased to hear doctors waxing poetic about crystals and plant medicine. Preferring natural means of healing, I remembered being ridiculed for refusing to take acetaminophen.

"On old Earth," said Ronan, "we are taught that chemical medicine is the only way to manage illness. There is no acknowledgement of the innate wisdom of the body. Humans continue to get sicker as we write more and more prescriptions. We are merely appeasing symptoms and not getting to the root of the problem. Of course, in an emergency, there is nothing better, and we save countless lives with your 'barbaric' techniques." Ronan glanced at Azriel. "Dense bodies, heavily traumatized, require dense medicine."

Soaking up the warmth of the sun, heavy memories fell like a weight upon our small party. Several small birds landed in the grass nearby and we all watched as they pecked and played before flying off into the clear blue sky.

"It is true, dense bodies require dense medicine," repeated Azriel with a sad smile. "However, now there is so much corruption and greed. The profound and ancient healing modalities are disregarded and even belittled instead of investigated and utilized. Many more lives could be saved if these techniques were incorporated."

"We have so much power within to heal," said Oriane. "I have often wondered why humans so easily consider the placebo effect something to be dismissed rather than harnessed. Is it not evidence that we have everything we need to overcome any illness?"

Ronan grinned, "Clearly, even my beloved plants pale in comparison to the power we hold within. The mind still believes it needs something external to heal, and so, I delight in offering my plants. I am not yet ready to give up this beautiful art. But, yes, one day soon, Healers will not be needed at all."

"It seems on old Earth," Azriel swallowed a bit of fruit, "there is a strong need for control. In medical school we are taught, 'first do no harm,' but great harm is often ignored and even buried. And now, humans are being threatened or shamed if they choose not to participate. Even a miracle of modern medicine cannot be helpful if forced upon a body. All forms of medicine are only beneficial when offered with love and pure intent, not through coercion and manipulation."

Ronan winced at Azriel's words and Oriane looked down, shaking her head.

"Control over the sovereignty of others is always toxic and can never bring health and healing," she said.

CHAPTER SIXTEEN

The Radiant Domes

*Everything in Elysia is built in harmony with nature, and there is no trash. . . **none**.*

Departing Harmony Healing Center, we enjoyed the warm afternoon sun. Oriane talked about the rapid growth of Unity and the formation of new polycenters. I half listened as I watched a group of Luminoles play a strange game with a flying object.

"They are practicing telekinesis," said Oriane, interrupting her own train of thought, "anyway, the Leaders of Elysia are very helpful when Luminoles want to start a new polycenter."

"Leaders?" I asked, surprised to hear that word. "Is there a political system here?"

"Sort of," said Oriane. "Unity is still in its infancy and Leaders harmonize the many new energies. As we evolve, the need for Leaders diminishes."

"So are Leaders. . . elected?" I asked doubtfully.

"No," said Oriane. "Just like everyone here in Unity, the Leaders must discover their inherent qualities. Once it becomes apparent that someone is gifted as a Leader, they are acknowledged by the community."

I grimaced remembering the leaders of old Earth, the lavish lifestyles, fancy private airplanes, envoys of limousines, and, of course, the air of self-importance that I found so disdainful.

"A true leader is simply a person who is skilled at listening to many voices at one time," she said. "There is no hierarchy among the Leaders here in Unity, only various levels of skill. They live like everyone else, and do not make laws nor do they seek to control. Real Leaders are rarely found on old Earth and never in positions of power."

Curious to meet these Leaders, I jumped in surprise when I saw two stunning Luminoles appear before me; a man and woman, both wearing regal deep purple robes with gold trim. Catching Oriane's thought, I understood that they had teleported to us instantly.

"I am Aziza," said the woman, "and this is my bond-mate Imani."

She had strong, distinct features and dozens of long dark braids cascading to her waist. She wore many long necklaces and extensive jewels.

"Welcome to the Central Hub of Elysia," she said. "We always enjoy meeting newcomers."

Imani, standing at her side, towered in stature. He had a shiny bald head and distant brown eyes. They had an air of royalty, and I felt an odd urge to curtsy or bow.

"Leaders tend to have well-developed telepathic skills," said Oriane.

"That is true," said Aziza. "However, Akashi also keeps us informed when newcomers arrive."

"I'm curious, if I may ask," I said, bowing my head in respect, looking down. "How did you become Leaders of Elysia?"

"Please," Aziza said. She touched my chin gently encouraging me to look in her large brown eyes. "There is no need for formalities. We are equals. There is always an adjustment coming from old Earth."

Imani answered my question. "We lived as members of the ruling elite in central Africa," he said. "After a bloody coup, we were ousted and imprisoned.

"Like most Luminoles, it was through our suffering that we came to understand the nature of true leadership. Once the population of Unity reaches maximum capacity, our role will no longer be necessary, and we will organically channel our skills into other areas."

I was impressed with Imani's matter-of-fact acceptance. On old Earth, very few people would give up their position of power without a fight.

"Unlike the leaders of old Earth," he said, "we do not perpetuate the delusion of infinite growth on a finite planet. We recognize the laws of nature. All life forms go through a natural cycle of birth, maturity, and eventually, death."

"Unity is in a period of rapid growth," said Aziza. "At some point, this realm will reach its natural maximum capacity. Births and deaths will spontaneously become equal. After a time of internal growth and development, there will be a natural time of decline. Eventually, when Unity has served its purpose, this world too, will die."

"I would like to spend some time here," I said.

"Of course," said Aziza. "You will find space in one of the apartment towers. Akashi will help you find an appropriate room. Take as much time as you wish."

Before evaporating, Aziza said, "Please come participate in a session whenever you like. Akashi will inform you of our whereabouts and you are always welcome."

I walked Oriane to The Whisper. After warm hugs, Oriane returned to her family in Azure Village and I stood alone, staring around at my new playground.

* * *

I easily found an open apartment with the assistance of an Akashi kiosk. My apartment, with a window in the place of one wall, was situated on the eighty-eighth floor of a spiraling high-rise and opened out to a patio overlooking the Central Hub.

Looking down upon the polycenter, I watched hovercrafts skim noiselessly over the glowing night lights of Elysia. A soft breeze tickled my face as I breathed in the night air.

I requested a bowl of soup from Akashi, and one arrived at my doorstep seconds later. The canopy of the round bed spiraled in a tree-like fashion to the ceiling, and I floated in my large warm waterfall pool before snuggling into the soft depths of my velvety new sleeping area.

The next morning, while enjoying bobbifruit; a new pale-orange delight that I had just discovered, I questioned Akashi about teleportation.

"Eighty-five Luminoles of Unity have developed the skill of teleportation," she said. "At this time, they can only teleport within the confines of their polycenter. Eventually, all Luminoles will be able to teleport to any location they wish."

Exploring the Central Hub of Elysia, I enjoyed the hum of activity. I never cared much for the cities of old Earth, preferring rural landscapes and quaint towns. But everything here was so fascinating and different, it was like a magical chocolate shop.

When I came across a group of Luminoles painting with some unusually vibrant colors, I looked on with interest. They immediately set me up with an easel and I got some excellent instruction on painting technique.

I sampled delicious and unusual treats available everywhere; star-shaped hors d'oeuvres, rich umami soups spiced with salty seaweed, and desserts of sweet fruits decorated with tiny button flowers.

A Culinary Creative with a small child-like body and extremely short, electric-purple hair held out a tray of pastries with tattooed forearms.

"I'm Sasha," she bounced up and down with a wide grin. "I made zis from sweet bark of a tree I found at zee mountain base."

She had a sparkling bejeweled lip ring attached to a chain from the left ear and a thick French accent. The delicious-looking delicacies were too tempting, and I tried one.

"Do you like it?" Sasha inspected my face as I took a bite and the flavorful melty softness exploded in my mouth. My new friend jumped and squealed. "Oh, I'm so happy zat you like it!" she said. Setting her tray on a bench, she rolled her pink sleeves further, exposing flowers and vines that covered both arms. She appeared to prepare for a detailed explanation.

"You see, I was able to grind up zee bark like flour and bake it with cacao beans and dates. On old Earth, I lived in Paris, and I ran a bakery. I wanted to see if I could create something like zis but not unhealthy, and zis is what I did. I'm going to share zis with Akashi and guess what?" she said grinning ear to ear. "Zee Builders are coming today to construct my new cafe."

Sasha pointed to an open storefront with a large glass window behind us. "It will have a kitchen, and lovely chairs and tables for everyone to sit and enjoy, just like in Paris."

"That sounds amazing," I said, genuinely happy for this little sprite. Her enthusiasm was infectious, but I was distracted.

"Hey, maybe you can help me," I said. "I'm new here and I used to love going in and out of shops on old Earth. There doesn't seem to be anything like that here."

"Oh, you want to go to zee radiant domes," said Sasha nodding her head and pointing towards the heart of the polycenter. "Zat is where everything happens."

* * *

"The closest radiant dome can be found a mile from the Zephyr." Akashi responded to my inquiry later that evening as I floated in the bath. She generated a map in the hologram.

I got out of the bath and wrapped myself in a cozy pink robe to get a closer look. I saw a rounded building that looked familiar, with a trail dotting from my apartment and then another to the radiant domes. Inspecting the map, I mentally planned my visit, which, according to Akashi, was only a two-and-a-half-mile walk.

I remembered Alaysia talking about the domes but really had no idea what to expect. I didn't want Akashi to spoil the surprise, so cut it off mid-sentence before the detailed description.

Up early the next day, I stepped onto my patio with a warm cup of chicory tea and breathed in the quiet sweetness of the wee morning hours. Off in the distance, I saw the glow of the Zephyr. The tip of a pyramid peeked out of a donut-shaped structure. I knew that *that* was the heart of the polycenter. I looked further but couldn't see the domes from my patio. Excited for the day, I dressed quickly. I enjoyed my stroll, helping myself to an enticing starfruit-filled pastry from another early-bird Luminole.

As I approached the Zephyr, I felt a strange, compelling force radiating from the structure. On the outside, it looked like a large water tank with a couple of doors. I knew from Akashi that it was open in the middle and contained a crystal pyramid.

Intrigued, as I passed, I made a mental note to check it out on another day. Today was Radiant Dome Day and I was looking forward to seeing how things were manufactured in Elysia. I chuckled to myself as I thought of all the changes I had been through in the past few months, never in my life on old Earth had I ever been interested in manufacturing.

After passing the heart of Elysia, I could see many large domes in the distance, not as large as the Zephyr, but many times bigger than my tiny home. My curiosity grew as I gravitated towards one constructed of a thousand triangles of glass, sparkling in the light, and figured it must be about five stories tall.

Entering the dome, the air was thick with warm humidity and filled with the earthy scent of rich compost. Ladened with trees resembling bamboo, the structure was teeming with life. Immersing myself in the sounds of chirping insects, rustling leaves, and bird calls, I navigated the lush foliage to find an Akashi kiosk.

The helpful hologram informed me that this dome housed aetherwood trees—a hybrid of bamboo and palm. Standing at the center, a large stabilizing post ran up the middle and generated a fine mist. The trees, soft and smooth to the touch, were capped with leaves and made pleasant clacking noises when they moved.

Luminoles were hovering silently or quietly holding their hands on the trees. I thought of Samita as I saw a familiar mass of curly hair. The person turned around and looked at me; Samita brightened and ran into my arms.

"Rose, I'm so happy to see you!" she exclaimed out loud. Delighted to see my friend, we hugged and shared silent gratitude.

"Did you ever think you would see me in a city?" she gushed with enthusiasm. "I'm living here now, working in *manufacturing* and. . . wearing clothes." She looked down at her tunic and shook her head. "I finally found my calling." She had tears in her eyes.

Samita showed me around and explained all about the domes and the creation of new stuff.

"Everything in Elysia is built in harmony with nature, and there is no trash. . . *none*," she said. "Everything gets reused or composted, and no landfills. Not like old Earth, where they pretend to recycle; it really happens here, no waste, *ever*. I'm here to see it firsthand. Really, this is healing me at the deepest level. It's beyond anything I could've ever imagined.

"Watch! I have to show you something." Samita wrapped her arms around one of the tallest trees. "This one is fully grown and ready to let go," she said, holding on. Samita closed her eyes and entered a trance-like state. After about fifteen minutes of silence, the tree gently fell into her arms and three awaiting Builders took it out of her hands.

"I just talked to the tree fairies and all the little worms and bacteria in the soil. The tree was ready to let go and with the help of the organisms, it released its roots so we could use it. That tree already made some babies, so now there's space for them to grow. On old Earth, I always dreamed about something like this, and now I'm making it happen. I'm happier than I've ever been. Thank you for being my friend."

She hugged me again and my heart felt so light and uplifted to see Samita in so much joy. Sometimes, as I walked around Elysia, I felt my heart might burst, and this was definitely one of those moments.

Making my way to the exit of the dome, I looked up at a platform and saw Peretz, Oriane's bond-mate. Wearing his regal burgundy robe, he was in deep discussion with another Luminole. They were studying a hologram and Peretz manipulated the design as he spoke. I gathered they were discussing new systems of self-cleaning technology that he, along with other Creatives, had developed. He pointed around at the aetherwood while sharing his ideas. The other Luminole nodded in agreement, offering suggestions on how to implement the new technology.

Peretz glanced at me with a warm smile before returning to his conversation. I stood for a moment, watching him work, trying to recall something that I quickly forgot.

When I entered the next radiant dome, much smaller than the last, I stepped into what would have been on old Earth, a chilling scene. Thousands of spiders busy at work, spun webs over a large metal gridwork. I explored, knowing with certainty that nothing in nature could harm me.

Luminoles sat quietly or gathered large swathes of fabric generated from the webs. Someone was sitting on a bench covered head to toe in spiders. Intrigued, I studied them intently and realized it was Alaysia. I had to squelch a sudden urge to pluck her from her perch. She opened her eyes and smiled.

"Hi," she said, looking elated. "I'm happy you finally came to see the radiant domes. Would you like to meet my friends?" She acted as if this were the most normal thing in the world.

I opened my mouth to speak but nothing came out. I had to quickly rearrange myself internally to accept what I was seeing. Samita, and everything she had taught me, was up for re-evaluation at that moment. I looked at Alaysia in wonder and awe. Her matter-of-fact acceptance of these usually feared creatures deepened my already profound respect for this young woman. My love for Alaysia was the catalyst that allowed me to relax all my defenses.

She must have sensed my readiness when she gently touched her fingers to mine. Before I knew it, the tiny arachnids covered my arm and were tickling under my tunic. I must admit, it was a test of my will that I was able to completely let go. After some time, I closed my eyes and tuned into the silent spider language.

A profound understanding dawned on me as the spiders shared their gifts and their skill. I knew I would never again deliberately kill one of these beautiful creatures.

* * *

Strolling in a gentle drizzle through Elysia, I puzzled once again at the intense familiarity that I felt with Peretz, Oriane, and Alaysia.

Glancing up, I saw Sasha running towards me in a brightly colored floral apron.

"Zee Builders just finished my new cafe, come see!" she breathed, and gave me a spontaneous squeeze. She showed me around the charming cafe handing me a croissant as I celebrated the new venture.

Back in my room, I floated in my tub while considering the day; the radiant domes, Samita, Alysia and the spiders, and Sasha's new cafe, built in a day. I imagined being able to share all the beauty and harmony of Elysia with the people of Earth and wondered if it was possible to show humanity a better way.

CHAPTER SEVENTEEN

The Zephyr

A true scientist must also be a mystic; always profoundly open to the realm of infinite possibility.

Crystalline technology is beyond anything found on old Earth." Waylan, a large man with chaotic blonde curls wearing an elegant blue robe had agreed to meet me at the Zephyr.

"I was a physicist and worked in nuclear energy," he said. "Even though it seemed like good, clean energy, I was always worried about the destructive forces. We used to think free energy was impossible." He paused, showing me to a door.

"You might want to take a breath. This is. . . *really cool*." He took a dramatic pause and pushed the handle down. Stepping through, he opened his arms, sweeping them upwards.

"Welcome to the Zephyr, the key to the crystal grid of Elysia!"

I froze, staring at an enormous crystal pyramid, and gasped. The shimmering tetrahedron ascended at least a hundred feet and emitted a soft, incandescent glow that seemed almost alive. Sparkles of sunlight dazzled off the massive structure, casting faint rainbows on the building encircling it.

"You feel that?" Waylan opened his palms and bit his lower lip. "If you slow down, you can feel the subtle pulse." He paused for a second and then, slowly opening and closing his hands, he mimicked the pulsation. "WoooM, WoooM, WoooM."

I closed my eyes and felt a subtle pleasant pulse fading in and out.

"Powerful stuff, eh?" he said. "Not like the old Earth EMFs that can make ya sick. Electromagnetics can mess up a body's electrical system, but not this."

I nodded remembering the annoying buzz of high-tension power lines and cell phone towers.

"Yup, hard to believe we rape the earth for its blood-oil and then dig up rare minerals like lithium and call it 'clean energy,'" he said, using air quotes. As we walked, Waylan expounded enthusiastically.

"This pyramid connects to the vast crystal grid and provides free energy to all Elysians. Every polycenter has a Zephyr like this and they link up, kinda like the internet. The extraterrestrials *finally* trusted us enough with their technology. If this becomes available on old Earth, *oh boy*—trust me, greedy men will misuse it."

"How does it work?" I asked.

"Well, this pyramid collects the energy of infinity which travels through the ley lines of our realm, hooking up with the grid."

"Wait, what is the energy of infinity? What does that even mean?"

Waylan stopped walking. "Just as you have energy in your legs that get you out of bed in the morning or—think of the energy in the tiniest seed to create the tallest redwood tree or a sun that lights up a thousand worlds. We can access this power." He paused to see if I was following, and continued walking.

I furrowed my brow trying to understand. Waylan pulled up an Akashi hologram and started writing complex mathematical equations.

"This is really simple math," he said. "I'm sure you can follow." Furiously he wrote exponents, binominals, and variables into the air, explaining the physics of crystal technology. As he droned on, I could no longer keep up.

Looking around, a glowing panel caught my eye. Reminded of a mandala, I had to take a closer look. Several Luminoles were leaning over a panel of glowing crystals in an exquisite geometric pattern.

"Oh," said Waylan, erasing the hologram and following me. "These are my colleagues, Hiroshi, Bakta and Nebu."

Hiroshi glanced at me, waving his hand for a second, too absorbed in his work for cordial conversation. Next to him, Bakta and Nebu, two Pleiadians, turned around and stared at me intensely. A wave of nausea coupled with an odd floating sensation came over me. I closed my eyes, putting my hand to my face, and tried to will the sensation away.

A brush on my shoulder made me look up; one of the blue beings had touched me. Hiroshi glanced up from the crystalline panel and then did a double take before handing me a glass of water.

"Oh, you're affected by the high vibration," he said. "Drink! I sometimes feel like I'm about to fly off Unity when I'm working with the extraterrestrials." Hiroshi put his hand on my shoulder for a moment before returning to the object of his obsession.

I drank the entire glass and after a moment the sensation passed.

"Occupational hazard," Waylan said with a chuckle, "anyway, as I was saying. . . "

We continued our walk and, still slightly dizzy from the encounter, I only half heard Waylan's explanation of the intricacies of the crystal grid.

After a time, Waylan turned towards the Zephyr, hands on his hips, gazing in fondness, and said, "Free energy affords us the ability to explore the endless ever-changing nature of reality."

Surprised, I glanced at Waylan and asked, "Wait, you're a scientist, don't you believe in the scientific method? Don't you believe there *is* an objective reality that you can study so you can know how the world works?"

"Of course," Waylan's face lit up, "the scientific method is a crucial tool. If followed meticulously, we *actually* discover the malleable nature of everything.

"You see, Rose, truths are constantly changing; the Earth was flat and then it was round and now. . . apparently, it's become flat again," he chuckled. "For a time, demons caused disease and then germs, and now we know microorganisms are friends, not foes. See what I mean?"

I nodded, not entirely confident, but did my best to grasp his words.

"Unfortunately, on old Earth, scientists willing to challenge the status quo are usually ridiculed, shunned, or even killed. It's too bad really, because it just limits our potential. If they want to keep their jobs, most scientists are forced to manipulate the scientific method to maintain old beliefs. *That* is what gets funded and published in the journals. Money corrupts everything," he said, shaking his head.

“I’m glad we don’t have to deal with that B.S. anymore,” he said under his breath then glanced at me. “S’cuse my French. Anyhoo, worn out science is offered as proof of the fixed nature of reality, so sad.”

Stopping our walk, we stood side-by-side and looked at the shimmering clear crystal pyramid. Waylan put his hands on his hips and nodded.

“A true scientist must also be a mystic,” he said, “always profoundly open to the realm of infinite possibility.”

CHAPTER EIGHTEEN

Leadership

In Unity, the Leaders have no agenda, our only purpose is to discover the will of the Luminoles for the highest good of all.

Aziza and Imani were working with a group of newcomers who wished to build a polycenter. I planned to join them. Happily strolling on a lovely morning, I paused for a croissant and chicory tea, giving Sasha a hug.

The group of thirteen, already gathered in a courtyard of fountains and archways, opened their circle and welcomed me in. With Aziza on one side and Imani, the other, I took my place between the two Leaders.

"Ten Luminoles have expressed the desire to create a new polycenter," said Aziza. "Four neutral parties stand at each corner to assist your process." She nodded in my direction and then at another Luminole standing opposite me. I squirmed, realizing that I was about to be a part of this process and not just a casual observer.

"The purpose of this gathering is to discover the nature of your polycenter, the site of your crystal grid, and basic design. Each of you holds extraordinary gifts, some yet unknown, and each contribution is of equal significance."

Aziza looked at Imani, and everyone turned their heads towards him. Imani held a stick in his hand.

"We stand," he said, "stationed in the four directions and create a stabilizing force." He held up the stick wrapped in leather, with hanging beaded tassels. "This is a talking stick, when you hold the stick in your hand, you command the attention of the group. Effective communication is crucial for amplifying your collective vision. The constructive collaboration of your efforts will surpass any individual capabilities."

All the Luminoles nodded and smiled, whispering amongst themselves. Imani took a breath, and everyone focused on him. As the stick went around the circle, I did my best to actively listen and support the group. When each Luminole spoke, they shared their vision, desires, and needs. All were heard and together they designed a polycenter beyond their wildest dreams.

As the process unfolded, my mind drifted to old Earth; the constant battles, negotiations, conflicts, and simmering tensions. It was a world where everyone screamed to be heard and no one listened. In contrast, this approach was so simple, joyful, and fruitful that I couldn't help but wonder why anyone would choose a different path. The outcome was so much greater than any one person could imagine, and every need was not just met, but exceeded beyond all expectations.

When the meeting adjourned, the Luminoles departed, taking their designs to the Builders; Imani left to talk with the newest Leader. Aziza and I sat by the fountain, enjoying the cool water, and I shared my thoughts about old Earth. Contemplating thoughtfully, she arranged her braids behind her and slowly interlaced her fingers before offering her insight.

"On old Earth," she said, "there is constant fighting between political sides. This ultimately serves as a distraction from the distorted, and often diabolical, intentions of those-that-seek-to-control." She paused, apparently lost in a painful memory.

"I know this because Imani and I were a part of this system, blinded by greed and power. Everyone supported our intentions until we were eventually held accountable for our destructive behavior. When we learned the truth, it was very painful. But I can now say that I have never been more grateful.

"In Unity, the Leaders have no agenda, our only purpose is to discover the will of the Luminoles for the highest good of all."

Humbled by her profound insight, I thanked her for her honesty. Hearing a Leader speak this way was a balm for my heart. After a warm hug she teleported away, leaving me to my thoughts.

Savoring a drink of the cool, crystal waters, I stared into the fiery sunset. Aziza made it seem so simple; no voting or fighting for the right leader. Hundreds of years of division, 'us-versus-them,' effortlessly tossed away with a mere flash of deep wisdom.

CHAPTER NINETEEN

Exploring Unity

Everything is energy. As we evolve, we tap into the field of infinite possibility.

Spending happy days, I explored everything. Discovering many different radiant domes, each with exquisite new materials and innovative designs, small cafes with culinary treats, and little pockets of exquisite artistry, I enjoyed all the delights the Central Hub of Elysia had to offer.

At Harmony Healing Center, Ronan expounded on the many uses of plant medicine. I spent hours wandering the greenhouse, trying unsuccessfully to contact the fairies. Watching Ronan make potions one day, he handed me a nutshell filled with salve.

"This can soothe deep pain," he said. "Take it, you might just need it." I put it in the pocket of my dress wondering what he meant.

Azriel handed me various gemstones explaining their attributes with great enthusiasm. Surrounded by crystals, I meditated on the subtle vibrations, until he placed a giant amethyst skull on my lap. Gazing at the remarkable treasure, I was so lost in its exquisite beauty that I barely heard Azriel's wisdom as he shared its deep secrets.

When I wasn't at Harmony Healing Center, exploring the radiant domes or discovering some new artistic craft, I joined Sasha in the café learning how to make delicious pastries. Together, we offered taste tests to those passing by.

Makai Ola Island

One day when Sasha and I were coming up with ideas for a cream-filled croissant, Sasha casually mentioned that she was leaving the next day for the tropical paradise of Makai Ola Island. Intrigued, I got the low-down from Akashi.

"There are currently fifty-three polycenters in Unity, all at various stages in their development. As each new polycenter is born, Luminoles with a vibrational match naturally gravitate and grow the population. Makai Ola Island is a relatively new polycenter modeled after the Hawaiian Islands of old Earth."

Enticed by the images of tropical Makai Ola, I decided to join Sasha. We convened at the hovercraft landing the next morning. Sitting in a comfortable reclining seat, all facing into the center of a circle, twelve travelers passed around the delicacies Sasha had brought aboard to share.

As we approached our destination, the floor of the vessel became transparent. I gasped looking at the tropical paradise below. The island, lush and green, was surrounded by white-sand beaches and turquoise waters with a majestic volcano at its center. My belly fluttered with excitement as we swiftly and silently descended.

We disembarked at a discreet landing port and the warm tropical breezes of Makai Ola greeted us. Appreciating the contrast with the drier, more temperate climate of Elysia, we donned colorful sundresses and grass sandals and began our adventures.

Sasha dashed off to uncover secrets of the tropical cuisine. I wandered to a pristine turquoise beach, finding a hammock in the shade under a palm tree. Watching the waves crash on the beach, I fell into a deep reverie. Recalling my fondness for the beaches of Hawaii, I smiled, grateful that here in Unity, I could enjoy all the pleasures of old Earth with none of the pain.

While Sasha was learning about new recipes for coconut, papaya, and guava, I leisurely relaxed in a straw bungalow chatting with a large, tattooed Culinary Creative named Nalu, who attempted to concoct a drink that matched my personality exactly.

"It's called Purple Sunrise," he said proudly, wiping his hands on his floral sarong. A parrot landed next to me, and I stroked its head, gazing at my surroundings.

Watching my face intently, Nalu encouraged me to take a sip. In front of me sat a large glass of deep purple liquid, lightly stirred with brilliant orange, complete with a tiny umbrella made of rice paper. Taking a sip of my Purple Sunrise, a tingling sensation came over me, and a sense of joy laced with peace and calm. I looked up at Nalu and smiled.

"I knew it!" Nalu slapped the counter with glee. "Purple star-fruit, passion, guava. I knew that was the ticket." He dashed off to create more drinks for other Luminoles.

Finishing my cocktail, I sighed with contentment. Nalu who, having just hit the mark on his latest customer, asked if I needed anything else.

"No thank you," I said. "By the way, where is your crys-tal pyramid?"

"Oh," he said, "the Zephyr is in the volcano." He pointed to a peak in the center of the island. "A Creative Leader, who lives in the polycenter of Shumba-La, helped install it. He was one of the first-comers here and has *incredible* powers. He and the eleventh-dimensionals suspended our crystal pyramid in the crater of the volcano. It hovers, just above the lava and gathers energy from the fiery flows."

I shaded my eyes with my hand peering up at the volcanic peak, remembering the destruction I had seen in the Hawaiian Islands from the many eruptions over the years.

"The Nature Protectors talk to the lava," he said. "They direct the flows to the sea, so we get the benefit of the power without the destructive effects. The volcano builds the island and expands our polycenter. We haven't reached maximum capacity yet, but I think we will soon, lots of new Luminoles are arriving every day." Nalu smiled a huge grin and seemed delighted at the idea of Luminoles loving the island as much as he did.

That evening in our grass hut, I wanted to talk to Sasha about what I had learned, but she was too excited to focus.

"I want to take all my new recipes to another polycenter. It's called Cote d'Azur Ville, designed to look just like Paris," she squealed. "One of zee Luminoles zer is starting a café. I want to help zem, and learn more too."

Sasha's enthusiasm inspired me and as much as I was enjoying my hammock on the beach, the thought of sitting in a Parisian café enticed me on to our next adventure.

Cote d'Azur Ville

Departing the next morning, we took a three-hour hovercraft ride to Cote d'Azur Ville. Parisian music filled our ears and the sweet scent of fresh pastries wafted as we wandered the cobblestone streets. Coming upon Sasha's friends, she fell into a frenzy of sharing recipes and innovative ideas.

I wandered through the polycenter enjoying all the sights and sounds of Paris. Viewing a structure reminiscent of the Eiffel Tower in the distance, a friendly Luminole told me it was called Tower Tiefel. I sipped a chicory cappuccino at a sidewalk table taking delight in the French chatter of the Luminoles sitting next to me.

I marveled at how I could be in Elysia one day, on a tropical beach the next, and sitting in a Parisian café two days later: no passport, no customs, and no stressful travel. I remembered reading fantasy novels on old Earth of people teleporting and always thought it would be amazing. I laughed aloud, shaking my head. If only the people of old Earth could see this.

Sasha ran up to me. "I'm returning to Elysia tonight," she said. She was panting heavily, arms full of hazelnut flour and vanilla beans. "I need to bring all zee new flavors and foods back to my café." After a quick hug, she requested a bag from Akashi and left.

I spent a few more days exploring the Parisian polycenter. Many Luminoles walked about naked, and no one gave them a second thought. At the top of Tower Teifel, I gazed around Cote d'Azur Ville. I saw the Zephyr peering out like a beacon in the distance.

Like all crystal pyramids, the Zephyr was stationed at the heart of Cote d'Azur Ville. It was surrounded by a building resembling the Louvre of Paris. I went in and gazed upon the many works of art generated by Akashi. Even knowing it wasn't the original, I still appreciated looking upon the Mona Lisa for the first time.

* * *

I visited several more polycenters, each one unique in its creativity and imagination. Everything I could imagine that brought joy on old Earth was at my fingertips. The languages of old Earth were alive for the enjoyment of the beautiful sounds. As in Elysia, every Luminole was welcoming, generous, and loving. My new world was a virtual utopia of unimaginable proportion. After a venture around a Japanese polycenter, I felt the niggling desire to return to Azure Village. But, before I did, I had one more stop to make on my adventures throughout Unity.

Shumba-La

A large dome opened as my hovercraft to Shumba-La landed. I was furnished with thick ivory furs that self-generated warmth. Exiting the now fully enclosed landing dome, I eagerly searched for the Luminole I yearned to meet. With the help of a sherpa, on the back of a yak, I trekked up a snowy mountainside, gazing at the towering, frozen peaks. As much as I dislike the cold, I eagerly anticipated my visit with this intriguing Luminole.

Finding the appropriate cave, I ducked in and settled myself quietly next to a bald elder. Chokyi appeared to be in deep meditation. Having been a Tibetan Monk on old Earth, he was highly sought after for his wisdom and insight. He had retreated to a Himalayan cave upon completing his mission on Earth and effortlessly ascended to Unity. Joining with the Pleiadians, he had prepared the realm for the arrival of the many new Luminoles.

Opening his eyes softly, Chokyi gazed at something invisible in the space. His demeanor was palpably calm and reassuring. He poured two cups of tea.

"Everything is energy," he said slowly. "As we evolve, we tap into the field of infinite possibility and eventually develop the power to create something out of nothing." He looked directly into my eyes.

"On old Earth, those-that-seek-to-control made you believe that reality is fixed and limited. They told you that you could never break free from your small little life and tried to convince you to give them your power in exchange for a few small crumbs of safety and occasional moments of pleasure."

We sipped tea and I smiled shyly over my teacup. After some time, he said, "You wish for me to manifest something, don't you?"

I blushed and looked down, embarrassed, "Yes, very much so please," I said.

"For you, my dear Rose, I would manifest anything," he said.

I blushed again, this time with pleasure as Chokyi fell into a deep trance. His face was focused and tranquil as he held out his hand. I watched intently, noticing nothing at first. Then an almost imperceptible haze appeared on his palm. I imagined a warm buzzing in my own hand as I dared not blink. Slowly, I detected an outline of an object which solidified and then materialized in his open palm.

I laughed aloud, letting loose an audible, "Huh!"

He smiled, apparently pleased with my delight. Chokyi brought into being a teacup, a beautiful candle holder, and remarkably, a small bowl of sweet rice pudding that we shared. It was delicious.

I was aware he could manifest much larger things if he wished, but he cautioned me.

"My dearest Rose," he said, "it is apparent to me that you understand true magic is the healing of the heart." I barely nodded, wanting him to continue.

"Lost souls only see the magic, desiring its power for selfish gain. For this reason, I rarely shared my gifts with those of old Earth, and when I did, it was only to ignite the desire to awaken. You understand this, as do all Luminoles, and thus there is no danger in augmenting our spiritual powers. When we recognize our magnificence, as well as the magnificence of others, we then have access to all the great powers we had lost and can utilize them for the benefit of all." He paused and I breathed in his words; for a moment my mind was still.

"When Unity reaches maximum capacity, we will then rapidly begin to expand our gifts, including that of instant manifestation. All Luminoles will develop this power."

Several days later, I met with Chokyi at the education center in an outland village of Shumba-La. A group of young children gathered around the elder with focused attention. Chokyi spoke of the phenomenal creative power that we all hold within. He spoke of the possibility of creating, not just small teacups, but also wonders of nature, fantastical structures, inspiring cities, and even worlds. The receptivity of these children moved me deeply. These children had all been born into Unity and as such, they had no concept of limitation.

I watched their little faces as they sat in calm serenity. The wise elder walked them through a simple lesson of manifesting small items in the palms of their hands. After the lesson, the children jumped up and ran to a steaming pool of hot water nestled into a snowy cleft. Splashing in joy, they were completely oblivious to the fact that they had just performed a miraculous feat.

I realized that these children had never known fear, greed, or suffering. These were the children born of Unity, and they were in no danger of growing up in a world of violence. As I watched them play, I imagined all the possibilities that could come from a child that was not wounded by life, but instead nurtured, protected, cared for, and valued. As I gazed around at the magnificence of Unity, I felt such a sense of hope for the future, all Luminoles and, in truth, all beings in all worlds everywhere.

* * *

After my journey through Unity, I knew that it would take me a thousand lifetimes before I became bored with my explorations. There was so much to see, do, and try. There were endless wonders, but for now, I was content to return to my humble village where my friends were waiting to welcome me home.

CHAPTER TWENTY

The Birth of Viviana

In a world of infinite possibility, I wondered why anyone would ever choose limitation and lack over kindness and abundance for all.

"Oh wow!" Malika stood up from the sofa and put her cup of chai down on the table. "You just answered my question."

Returning home, I had spent several days of quiet contemplation in my cozy dome before seeking out Malika to share my adventures.

She bounced up and down on her toes looking around. She had been listening intently to my descriptions and appeared to have had an epiphany. I was having trouble discerning her thoughts.

"Your description of the Central Hub and Unity inspired me," she said, filling me in. "I'm gonna do it!"

"Do what?" I asked, still in the dark.

She sat down and took my hands. "I'm going to move to the Central Hub and learn creative building," she said, practically glowing.

"Wow, that's incredible." I was genuinely excited for her. "You just decided that—just now?"

"Well, I had been thinking about it for a while and have talked to Greta and Alfred," she said. "They had mentioned their mentor in the Central Hub. Your description of Elysia was the final piece, and now, I know. . . I am going to move there tomorrow."

She began gathering up her artwork and crystal mobiles, putting them in the closet and sending them to the CDC.

"Well, that was an easy decision." I smiled at her joy and watched her empty her small dome in preparation for the move.

"OH!" She suddenly put her hand to her face, and I knew she had been hit by yet another revelation.

"I'm not leaving tomorrow, I'm leaving *today*!" she said.

"Wait, what? Why?"

"Well, you know, I've been single for a *very* long time."

I nodded my head remembering old Earth and her need for solitude after a bad break-up.

"I'm now ready for a relationship," she said.

My mouth stood open for a second then closed. Before I could ask about dating in Unity, Malika belted out, "Akashi!" The hologram lit up with a glow. "I'm ready to meet my bond-mate."

After a moment, as if the hologram were thinking, Akashi responded. "Your bond-mate will meet you at the Central Hub's main Whisper platform later today, he will be arriving from Cote d'Azur Ville."

Malika laughed. "Of course! He's French! Je parle français, et j'aime Paris. Oh, good, I remember how to speak French."

After getting a few more details, Malika stopped Akashi from telling her everything. She wanted to explore her new bond-mate in person.

I walked her to the Whisper as she talked excitedly about her new life.

"He is a Creative too," she said, "and we can study creative building together, then we will live in Cote d'Azur Ville. It's perfect. I've always wanted to return to Paris. Oh, I'm so happy! Thank you for inspiring me."

She hugged me and I stuffed down a niggling sadness. I didn't wish to diminish the light of her discovery by sharing my heavy thoughts during her triumphant moment. Before she boarded the hovercraft, now floating just above our heads, she took my hands.

"You will find your place too, I know it," she said.

After the sudden goodbye, I figured a swim in Serene Lake would do me good. I slowly trudged through the heart of Azure Village on my way to the lake, watching the Luminoles going about their day. Cedar and Dara were practicing backflips together in the garden. Cedar spotted Dara as she tried to reach the ground with her hands. Puma was directing Jax to turn into a giant lizard and Akira was laughing as Jax morphed from lizard person to Jax and back again. The other children of Azure Village ran around screaming and laughing, while Alaysia's friend Chestnut chased them around.

I saw Veeda picking herbs with her middle son, Summit, and noticed her very swollen abdomen. I went to give her a hug and she looked up, herbs in hand, and warmly received me. Rubbing her belly, she shared her excitement.

"Any day now," she said. Summit put his ear to the baby and informed me that he could hear the heartbeat.

"I can't wait to meet Viviana," I said, feeling genuinely excited to see a newborn again.

After a vigorous swim in Serene Lake, I sat on the shore, listening to the gentle lapping of waves. Looking up at the sky and feeling the warmth of a soft breeze, I gave my grief some space to breathe. I thought of old Earth and my friends, the suffering, and the pain, and contemplated how we managed to create so much limitation and lack. In a world of infinite possibility, I wondered why anyone would ever choose that over kindness and abundance for all.

* * *

I woke in the middle of the night with an overwhelming desire to find Veeda. I grabbed Ronan's salve instinctively and ran out of the house. I found Veeda under a tree in the garden, squatting and swaying back and forth. I put my hands on her, gently rubbing the soothing herbal ointment onto her belly as she moaned and smiled.

When I got up to fetch her family, Veeda grabbed my arm, looked at me intently, and said, "No! just you."

I looked at her determined and sweaty face and I nodded.

"OK," I said softly, "Just us."

Together, we swayed and sang as I held her through her labor pains. She followed the rhythm of her body and moved from walking and squatting to lying down and moving again. As I softly serenaded her with my untrained voice, I suddenly looked up in surprise to see Grizzle sitting quietly nearby. The large beast got up and padded towards us. Lying behind Veeda, he offered his body as a pillow, and she relaxed into the mountains of fur. We became a team. I watched her breathe and enter a deep trance in the creation of new life.

As Viviana was about to make her appearance, Aspen, and all the men arrived. Providing soft blankets, they surrounded us in a protective circle. Viviana made her entry with a robust squawk before I helped her cocoon onto her mother's breast. Cedar placed a warming blanket he had designed over his new sister and Puma stared at the small being, obviously completely entranced.

Leaving the placenta to Grizzle, I stayed with Veeda and Viviana until they were safely tucked into the warmth of their bed. Aspen offered warm broth and Josiah and Baz shuffled the boys out so the tired momma and baby could rest. As I slowly made my way home in the soft light of dawn, a gentle rain began to fall, and I wondered why that had felt so natural.

I mentally concluded that my telepathic abilities had expanded considerably and figured that *that* must be the reason. I had been in tune with Veeda's needs and I naturally followed her rhythm. Tired, but also uplifted, I napped into the light of the morning.

CHAPTER TWENTY-ONE

My Innate Gifts

The power of your light and love bent time and space and healed the hearts of tens of thousands of people.

Visiting Viviana daily, I stacked pillows under Veeda's arms, so the baby could feed. A doting pack of boys drifting in and out of the dome ensured that every need the mom and babe could possibly have was met instantly. In the rare moments that I held Viviana in my arms, I swayed and sang to her. Marveling at her tiny delicate features, I was consumed by an overwhelming sadness that threatened to swallow me whole.

* * *

Late one morning after yoga and a naked swim in Serene Lake, I returned home to a buzz of excitement in the village. Magna had prepared a grand performance, and inhabitants of the Central Hub and surrounding villages of Elysia were joining us. Joyful fresh faces poured into Azure Village.

She was doing a show about the time of ciphervirus and Zeta. Those who had been traumatized came from far and wide for the much-needed healing of laughter. There were hugs of joy as we passed around merry-berry wine in an air of excitement and anticipation.

We all settled down as Magna's performance unfolded. In her usual Magna style, with great skill and compassion, she morphed and changed into hilarious and magnificent characters. Dara, Cedar, and all the children in the production ran around in mock fear as they piled more and more paper masks upon their faces, breathing on each other and falling in fits of giggles. The children begged for the strange green Magna authority figure to poke their skin over and over pretending to convince each other that the *next* poke would be the magical key to endless bliss.

In her extraordinary style, Magna took the seriousness of the ciphervirus and Zeta era and turned it into a hilarious play. Magna skillfully brought lightness to what had been a heavy and painful time for so many. She morphed and danced until we were all able to see with absolute clarity the ridiculousness of the old Earth way.

Jax's booming laughter filled the air and made it all the funnier. By the time the show was over, nearly everyone was laughing with tears rolling down their cheeks. I felt a heaviness lift from the crowd and a profound sense of peace descended.

As the crowd dispersed to dance, sing, and share merry-berry wine, I sat in silence. Akira, not wishing to participate in the show, sat quietly next to me cuddling a cat. She suddenly turned to me.

"Rose," she asked, "were people of old Earth really scared of each other's breath?"

I realized that I had been holding my breath and sighed with a sad smile. "Yes, they were," I said, "and they believed it so strongly."

She shook her head with sadness and said, "We humans on old Earth were so silly, weren't we?"

Observing the wisdom of a child, her eyes big and innocent, I nodded in agreement with some heaviness in my heart.

"Yes, we were. We really were," I said.

As Akira shrugged her shoulders and wandered off to play with the others, I set down my untouched glass of merry-berry wine and melted into a silent reverie.

I contemplated my final days on old Earth, remembering the intense fear of ciphervirus and Zeta. I thought of the injections, harsh treatments, the masking, and the sanctuary cities turned to death camps. I remembered the intensity of the fear for so many. The desire welled up to somehow reach all those fearful souls from my past and soothe them and help them to not be afraid. As I sat there, tears streamed down my face, and my desire intensified to the point that I had no choice but to reach out.

With all the power I could muster from within, I reached out to all the souls living in fear and dread. I felt my heart expand and my energy surround those crying scared souls. I saw all the people in the sanctuary cities cowering in their homes, wearing tight-fitting, formaldehyde-laden masks. I saw the scars from the injections that they had repeatedly received in hopes of relief. I saw mothers too afraid to hug their children and the faces of those who could not accept an embrace. My heart cried with compassion, and I longed to show the suffering people of old Earth a better way.

I wanted to show them the possibility of a world of love and peace, respect, and compassion. I beamed a vision of a world where children grow up without fear; where all needs are met, and all forms welcome. I shared, with the strength of my love, a world of unimaginable creativity and abundance, a world of Unity. My heart cried out to anyone who would listen. With every ounce of my being, I reached out to any soul who could hear me. I expanded my energy to cover the entire Earth with my love, compassion, and care. I sent waves of light and healing, oceans of peace and forgiveness.

I sat and I cried, and I prayed for the healing of old Earth. I prayed for nature and the animals, but most of all, I prayed that all fear be released and for all beings to remember their magnificence. I prayed for everyone to drop the toxic weapons, restore nature, hug each other, and laugh with me. Tears continued to stream down my face until I felt a subtle shift in the energy of the Earth.

My body relaxed and I slowly opened my eyes to see Oriane's radiantly glowing face before me. She reached out for my hand and beamed at me.

"What you just did, was the force that allowed you to awaken and arrive here, along with countless others. The power of your light and love bent time and space and healed the hearts of tens of thousands of people."

I breathed in awe of her words. "So that was real? I really was able to affect all those people from the past, and even myself?"

"Yes," said Oriane. "You are a very powerful Healer."

Suddenly, memories of my life on old Earth came flooding back; the years I'd spent as a hospital nurse in San Francisco, the hundreds of births I had attended, the countless hours of studying herbal medicine, hypnotherapy, trauma healing, acupuncture, and breath work. I remembered that I had never felt very effective on Earth, never felt what I had to offer was enough.

Then I recalled lifetimes of study; I had been a nurse in the Civil War and was burned during the Salem witch trials. I had spent lifetimes learning healing and I knew Oriane was right.

"With some additional training, your skills will grow rapidly," said Oriane.

I suddenly felt the overwhelming desire to help all the new Luminoles that were coming to Unity. "Tomorrow, I will meet with Maanya to begin my training," I said.

Oriane nodded. "She will be expecting you."

CHAPTER TWENTY-TWO

Oriane's Revelation

It was apparent that, together, we had created something miraculous.

The next day, I went to Crescent Healing Center to request training from Maanya. She was waiting for me with open arms. Greeting me warmly, we sat down, and she took my hands in hers.

"It is with immense joy that I sit here with you in recognition of the profound gifts you hold within," she said. "For, it is I that has been watching over you for many lifetimes."

I looked into her eyes, falling into her words and a recognition washed over me.

"Yes," Maanya said. "Welcome home my daughter, you thought I was gone, but I have never left."

My heart leapt with joy as I fell into Maanya's arms and knew the truth of her words. On old Earth, my mother had died, and I was left with a hole in my heart. She had been my anchor, my confidante, and my best friend. She had always been there, joyfully loving me, and when I thought she'd gone, I felt as if I'd never be whole again.

And now here she is, from the eleventh dimension, my healer, and my teacher. I sobbed happy tears as I received her love.

* * *

The following days were filled with joy and wonder. Maanya oversaw every aspect of my training. Skilled in the subtle arts of energy healing, she insisted that I first learn from Ronan and Nora, the physical healing modality of herbs. In the Central Hub, I made salves and tinctures and came to understand the energetics of the plant world. Maanya showed me the technologies that had been brought from the eleventh dimension, simple, yet powerful tools using sound and light, and Azriel guided me to use crystals to knit bones and heal wounds.

Maanya taught me the subtler healing techniques involving my hands and my energy field. She showed me how to gently, with permission, enter the field of another. I learned to communicate on a soul level, expanding or contracting my energy to provide the optimal healing environment. I gained insight into the healing powers of various colors and how to use them to provide the exact right healing.

I discussed with her the healing modalities on old Earth; the sterile, complicated operating rooms, the cutting open of bodies with knives, the insertion of objects, and chemical medicine with the many side effects, and she smiled.

"Yes, all those old Earth techniques had their place. Old Earth is a very dense, three-dimensional realm and thus requires very dense healing techniques. However, all those techniques fail to acknowledge that we are first energy; matter is secondary. As consciousness increases, we become much more receptive and responsive to gentler healing modalities."

I used herbs to heal open wounds; crystals and sound energy to knit broken bones; energy and light to shrink tumors. As more and more Luminoles arrived, my skills as a Healer grew.

After a time, Maanya informed me, "Healing open skin wounds, broken bones, and shrinking tumors is easy. Healing the wounds of the heart is far more difficult."

With every healing, Maanya skillfully guided me into the subtle wounds of the heart. I learned to detect pain, shame, guilt, and unworthiness. I felt the eons of lies and suffering that had been put upon humanity and slowly, my gifts expanded. Little by little, I was able to assist Luminoles to release the deep pains and sorrows lodged in their cellular structure.

* * *

"We have an important newcomer arriving tomorrow," said Maanya one day. "I believe this one will benefit from your energy and healing. He lived an exceedingly difficult life and has been shattered and bruised. He carries the heavy burden of shame and guilt. He has bravely learned through his suffering and released his fears, but his body still carries deep pain."

To prepare for the healing, Oriane, Nora, Miriam, and I joined together with Laanza, a Pleiadian. We sat in meditation together and telepathically communicated the various contributions we wished to make.

As the newest Luminole shimmered and appeared in the Cocoon, Laanza stood at the head, Oriane and I at the arms, and Nora and Miriam at the legs. Laanza guided the healing with skillful attention. Miriam started with a deep warm hum and filled the Cocoon with healing sounds. Nora energetically wrapped the newcomer in a motherly embrace. Oriane planted a seed of forgiveness in his heart, and I watered the seed with my love to help it grow.

Expanding the seed with my energetic intention, it filled the heart of the newcomer, pulsing out in all directions until he was vibrating a warm, golden glow. As the healing continued hour after hour, any crumb of resonance with the pain of the newcomer melted away from our collective energy field. I gazed at the sleeping soul, with half-open eyes, remaining in my deep healing trance, and suddenly realized who this person was.

The newcomer was the mayor of San Francisco, the one who had initiated the sanctuary city that later became the death camp that killed so many. As I reached my heart to touch his, I felt his guilt and his shame. I understood his deep desire to do good, and how greed and selfishness overtook him. After the horrors of the death camps, he had sunk into a deep depression and cowardly hid in a bunker during the war. He had so much guilt and shame that he could not eat the dwindling supplies that were offered to him. The cans of peaches and the freeze-dried food had gone untouched. In deep remorse, he had starved himself. As he got closer to his death, his heart cried out for mercy and, with the light streaming onto Earth, mercy was granted.

I knew he had natural talents as a Leader and saw all the good he would do here. I knew his journey as a dealer of death would serve him well. He had paved an iron-clad path for his soul to recognize the trap of pride, greed, and selfishness. His soul was here to start a new polycenter along with many, many of the victims of the death camps. They served each other in mysterious ways only their souls could understand.

After that healing, feeling alive and renewed, my desire to serve intensified. In the years that followed, I performed many, many healings. At Harmony Healing Center, we received the casualties of war, soldiers and civilians, victims and perpetrators, innocents, and betrayers. They all came for healing, forgiveness, and retribution. My knowledge grew, and the depth of my compassion for all beings solidified. I understood that we are *all* traveling on a unique journey, and *all* serve the divine mystery.

One evening as I walked through Azure Village, I looked up to see Oriane walking next to me. I looked into her eyes and saw the warm familiarity and a flash of almost recognition.

"Oriane, I'm still trying to understand how I know you, your husband, and your daughter," I said. "You are all so familiar to me. I feel there is something here that is important for me to understand. Do you know what I'm speaking of?"

Oriane looked at me with deep love and respect. "Because you asked, it is time that you know. You see, I am you and you are me, we are one and we are the same. Back on old Earth, we lived the same life. We had the same experiences and the same family. Peretz was our husband and Alaysia our daughter.

"However, during the time of ascension, we split into two. My consciousness chose to focus attention on the family, and you chose to become the master Healer that you are. It doesn't happen very often, but like everything else, anything is possible. Our healing gifts would not have expanded had you stayed with the family. But, of course, your heart would never abandon your loved ones, so our consciousness found a way to have both experiences."

My breath caught in my throat and images came rushing back from my life, *our* life. I breathed in deeply, and I breathed some more and hot tears welled up, tears of remembrance and tears of joy. The rush of knowing was beyond belief. A river streamed down my face without my fully understanding why. Oriane stood at my back and placed her hand on my heart and her other on my head. I melted into her body and the truth of what she was sharing. How could the impossible have happened without my knowing?

It was only through forgetting that I could have allowed this all to be. It was apparent that, together, we had created something miraculous. Just then, Peretz and Alaysia arrived and surrounded me with love, and we all cried the happy tears of reunion.

CHAPTER TWENTY-THREE

The Newest Luminole

Every being in this realm is essential and a vital key to the tapestry.

Altered by the revelation that had occurred, I stumbled to the Crescent to seek out Maanya. I found her standing, deep in reverie, gazing out the window into the wilderness and beyond. I joined her, wondering what she was seeing. After a time of silence, with a far-off voice, she started to speak.

"For the last few centuries, the entity called Earth has been going through an ascension process. Light has been pouring onto the planet in ever greater quantities year after year. In response to this vast influx of light, the darkness responds and grows as well. Because Earth is a planet of duality, the light and the dark must remain in balance at all times.

"As the Earth ascends, so do all the inhabitants. For the first time in the history of the world, humans have the opportunity to leave Earth via ascension versus death. As this light floods the Earth, more and more humans have access to the fifth dimension. They do so by expanding their energy field, releasing attachment to fear and judgment, and allowing their bodies to become lighter and less dense. At that point, duality collapses within their consciousness, and they discover the power of *choice.*

"Some of those beings choose to stay on Earth and assist the ascension of others, whereas others decide to depart to a more pleasant realm. Once you reach the fifth dimension you are no longer bound to the Earth, and most choose to leave.

"For many souls, great suffering is required to awaken the deep desire for wholeness. As the collapse of old Earth progresses, many more souls will wake up. There are still many who are not yet ready for the fifth dimension and yet can no longer call three-dimensional Earth their home due to its destruction. Those souls will find a new, even more dense three-dimensional home where they will continue to play out the necessary drama until they are ready to awaken.

"There is a divine perfection at play, which cannot be understood by the human mind. At all times, everything is in right order and there is never a need for fear.

"Currently, old Earth has descended into thermonuclear war, and the final card is about to be played. Those-that-seek-to-control are about to release their final weapon.

"At this time, all the extraterrestrials have left the Earth, but their technologies remain. Those-that-seek-to-control have discovered their crafts and their technologies and intend to use this information to unleash the final fear. They have reverse-engineered extraterrestrial spacecraft and developed the technology to simulate an alien invasion of Earth.

"They intend to spread mass fear to achieve their final goal, the weaponization of space. Once they have achieved their goal, they will use those weapons to strip the atmosphere which will then destroy all remaining life forms, leaving old Earth barren. This will be the final dramatic crescendo and the end of old Earth.

"We have a large group of new Luminoles that will arrive tomorrow, and your healing gifts are required."

* * *

Heeding Maanya's words, I prepared myself through meditation and solitude. I aligned myself with the various energies of the newcomers, expanding my compassion to allow myself to hold the intensity of their suffering. Arriving at Harmony in the Central Hub the next day, I prepared the space for the new Luminoles.

I stepped into the center of a circle of twelve Cocoons. Each one slowly filled with a newcomer lost in a deep trance. I held out my hands, took a breath, and opened my heart. Expanding my energy in twelve directions, I wrapped each one in a healing blanket of love and protection. Within this group was the President of the United States, a woman, who had been heralded as a hero and a champion for the rights of all women. She had been the one to initiate the first nuclear attack. She authorized the blast to take out Moscow under the guise of protecting the world from a mad dictator.

The others in the group were some of the victims of the blast, and all had ascended moments before their death. With my energy and their openness, together, we created a deep connection. Twelve souls rose to a point of light and together, they merged into a singularity of pure consciousness. For a flash, they became one before splitting back into twelve.

They understood the dance of light and dark and forgiveness was no longer required. They had fulfilled their purpose together on Earth and they were now ready for Unity.

* * *

Following the collective healing, I returned home. Floating in Serene Lake, I basked in the warm glow of the sun. After my swim, I joined Veeda and her family for a picnic. Viviana had grown and was ten years old and followed Puma everywhere. Puma, now a feisty, fiery fifteen-year-old, came up to me and plopped onto the beach blanket. He grilled me about the President and the healing I had just done. He wanted to know what had happened and why.

Not wanting to talk about old Earth, I told him I was tired. To his credit, he pretended to believe my excuse. Puma's inquisition gnawed at me, however, and a burning question arose. I would ask Maanya at our next meeting.

* * *

Maanya spoke clearly and slowly. "Unity was created by a small group of humans who experienced a deep desire for harmony, peace, and connection. Through the power of their intention, this realm came into being.

"My companions and I came from the eleventh dimension to assist. We were the first to arrive and helped those firstcomers build this world. Additionally, we reached out telepathically to all those on old Earth who are ready to ascend.

"The destruction of Earth is imminent. We have been preparing the land for the arrival and the final newcomers will complete the circle. As you reach maximum capacity you will all live in oneness and at that time, a great power will come over this entire realm. The collection of gifts and talents will form a whole and together, you will be greater than the sum of all the parts.

"As you bond with each other, you will begin to evolve at a faster pace. Your gifts will expand exponentially, and you will have greater and greater access to the realm of infinite possibility.

"At that point, my companions and I will leave, as you will no longer require our assistance. Every being in this realm is *essential* and a *vital key* to the tapestry."

* * *

That evening, as I relaxed in my shell bath with a warm cup of chocolate, sweet bark tea, I had a compelling impulse and planned to ask Maanya for guidance. A new Luminole was set to arrive in our community, and I felt a strong urge to be their welcoming guide.

"It is unusual for someone of your skill to be a welcoming guide," said Maanya thoughtfully. "But it is apparent that this newcomer will benefit greatly from your healing energy. This newcomer is of vital importance to the community and will need your assistance to acclimate and remember their gifts."

Maanya and I spent the remainder of the day aligning with the newcomer. Receiving their soul's permission, we investigated the history of their life journey; the pains and sorrows; needs and desires; and their gifts and talents. We went into Azure Village to find the ideal living situation and prepared the community for their arrival.

"This newcomer is very special," said Maanya again. "Their gifts will be of great assistance to the evolution of Unity. We are indeed blessed to have their presence among us. They will uplift our world in new and incredible ways."

There was palpable excitement in the village at the arrival of the newcomer. Everyone was prepared to welcome them, and we were excited to see how this new presence would enhance everyone. In eager anticipation that evening, four Healers and I sat together in silent connection to ready ourselves.

The following morning, I was standing in the same place where I had arrived ten years prior. I held the energy steady, and I supported our newest Luminole as best I could. I felt the energy expand as their body ascended from the horrors of old Earth. Waiting patiently for the process to complete, I watched the shimmering form slowly become solid. The excitement grew and my desire for reunion intensified. Finally, before me, appeared a magnificent human. I took a breath, waiting for what seemed like an eternity.

You opened your eyes and took a breath, staring at me.

I smiled warmly and said, "Welcome to Unity."

And *now*, the stories can begin. . .

**No snakes were harmed in the writing of this book.

History of Unity

Unity came into being roughly two-hundred years ago. It was seeded by a small band of humans who had a burning desire for peace and oneness. With the assistance of the eleventh-dimensional beings, they brought into form an Earth-like realm and called it Unity.

Starting with technologies gifted to them by the extraterrestrials, they built the first crystal grid in the realm and harnessed the power of free energy. With unlimited energy at their fingertips, the firstcomers built a fantastical polycenter. They then proceeded to reach out to all the inhabitants of old Earth, seeking those who were ready to live in oneness, and assisted them with their ascension.

The entity called Earth is in a powerful ascension process and an increasing amount of light is pouring onto the planet, slowly awakening the slumbering masses. As more people wake up to their divinity, they stream into the utopian realm. As Unity grows, so too, does the power and force of the light that is assisting Earth in her transition. Old Earth, being a planet of duality, is required to have an equal amount of darkness at all times; thus, under the laws of the universe, those-that-seek-to-control become ever more powerful and diabolical in their destruction of the planet.

As the opposing forces intensify, one by one, beings awaken and collapse duality, creating the possibility of choice. Upon awakening, they are no longer bound to old Earth and are free to stay and assist humanity or leave for a more pleasant realm.

Unity is currently in its infancy and a period of rapid growth. When Unity reaches maximum capacity, she will be at the point of maturity, and the next phase of existence will begin.

Glossary of Terms

Akashi: AI accessing Universal Divine Intelligence.

Azure Village: The small outland village of Elysia where Rose and her friends live.

Builder: A contribution to Unity. Builders work with their hands, building things. They are identified by their overalls and rompers.

Bond-mate: The chosen sexual partner or partners of the Luminoles of Unity. Bond-mates are either recognized or requested.

Central Hub: The nucleus of a polycenter.

Cote d'Azur Ville: A Parisian-like polycenter of Unity.

Creative: A contribution to Unity. Creatives access the field of infinite possibility, bringing forth innovative ideas. They are identified by their bright and playful colors.

Creative Builder: A Creative that expresses their gifts through innovative design.

Crescent: The healing center in Azure Village.

Crystal Grid: The free energy system of Unity. The grid consists of a crystal pyramid at the heart of every polycenter that connects with smaller crystal structures throughout.

Culinary Creative: A Creative that expresses their gifts through food.

Educator: A contribution to Unity. Educators share knowledge with others.

Elysia: One of the first polycenters of Unity and the home of Rose and Oriane.

Harmony Healing Center: The healing center in the Central Hub of Elysia.

Healer: A contribution to Unity. Healers assist with healing the physical body and releasing the trauma of old Earth.

Instant Manifestor: A Luminole that can manifest objects using the power of the mind.

Leader: A contribution to Unity. Leaders assist groups in harmonizing their energies and assist with the creation of new polycenters.

Luminoles: The inhabitants of Unity.

Makai Ola Island: A tropical polycenter of Unity.

Nature Protector: A contribution to Unity. Nature Protectors connect deeply with plants, animals and minerals and ensure that all actions performed in Unity are in accordance with the laws of nature. Identified by the magnetic draw of animals to them.

Polycenters: The cities of Unity.

Radiant Domes: The site of all manufacturing in Unity, located in the Central Hubs of the polycenters.

Shumba-La: A Tibetan-like polycenter of Unity.

The Whisper: The transportation system in Unity.

Zephyr: The crystal pyramid that lives at the heart of every polycenter.

Acknowledgements

Sri Mata Amritanandamayi Devi for giving me everything.

Paul, my husband, for being my rock.

Aysia, my daughter, for her boundless compassion and creativity.

Zev, for being the best dog in the whole-wide world.

Mom, for teaching me about the infinite nature of reality and filling my life with love.

Aunt Rita and Aunt Eileen, for filling the void in my heart with peace.

Monica, for being my best friend and igniting my creativity.

Samantha, for her irreverence and teaching me about composting poop.

Alan, for letting me talk and being willing to consider everything.

Darshana, for encouraging me to write this book.

Ivy, for her creative garden and loving presence.

Ruth Ann, for making the world a safer place.

Kimberley, for dancing gracefully through the challenge of single motherhood.

Kate, for crying with me in the realization of what we have done to Earth.

Katharina, for offering a safe place to share everything.

Penny, for practicing Ahimsa.

My grandchildren, Isaiah, Casiel, Kashaya, and Lilit, for bringing me joy.

Emily, Ben, Josh, and Cynthia, for welcoming me wholeheartedly into the family.

Scott, for bringing me Aysia and transmitting levity to the heaviness of the world.

My brothers, sisters-in-law, nieces, and nephews, for loving me no matter how weird I get.

Mis compañeras, for providing compassionate care to birthing people.

Catalina, for traveling with me to the fifth dimension.

Jess, for her open mind and heart.

Bobbi, for her dedication to natural birth.

Susannah, for agreeing with me that we're all doomed.

LGBTQ friends and family, for adding color and vibrancy to my life.

Kaya Sattva, for introducing me to my compassionate blue extraterrestrial.

Sophie, for informing me of the shenanigans of those-that-seek-to-control.

Fred Burks and wanttoknow.info, for bringing knowledge and light to the world.

Doctors Sam & Mark Bailey, Dr. Tom Cowan, Dr. Andy Kaufman, Alec Zeck, Dawn Lester & David Parker, and Amandha Vollmer, for tirelessly pointing out the insanity of germ theory.

Pablo Sender for skillfully helping me comprehend theosophical wisdom.

Professor Guy McPherson, Pauline Schneider, Kevin Hester, Paul Beckwith, Micheal Dowd, and Phillise Todd for waking me up to the dire nature of our predicament.

Fred Burks and Steven Greer for educating me about extraterrestrials and free energy.

To all brave scientists who are not afraid to challenge the status quo.

ABOUT THE AUTHOR:

Photo: Terri Motraghi

V.M. Elyse is a spiritual seeker and lover of truth. She lives in Northern California with her family, and this is her offering to the world. The Realm of Unity is her first book, but not her last.

Her most fervent wish is that this book brings more light, love and healing into this ailing world.

TheRealmOfUnity.com